FORTY MILES FROM POPLAR BLUFF

Margaret —
I treasure the time
I spent in your class.
Thank you.
Rachel

FORTY MILES FROM POPLAR BLUFF

Rachel J. Ross

Writers Club Press
San Jose New York Lincoln Shanghai

Forty Miles from Poplar Bluff

All Rights Reserved © 2002 by Rachel Jordan Ross

No part of this book may be reproduced or transmitted in any form or by any means, graphic, electronic, or mechanical, including photocopying, recording, taping, or by any information storage retrieval system, without the permission in writing from the publisher.

Writers Club Press
an imprint of iUniverse, Inc.

For information address:
iUniverse, Inc.
5220 S. 16th St., Suite 200
Lincoln, NE 68512
www.iuniverse.com

ISBN: 0-595-21661-7

Printed in the United States of America

To Grilla,
Life can be messy.

Contents

August 1
September 11
October 29
November 39
December 49
January 63
February 71
March 95
April 107
May 115
About the Author *121*

Acknowledgements

"The time for pie is when pie is passing."
—D. KIRKWOOD MARTIN

August

It was the tail end of *the* hottest summer on record in southeast Missouri, that summer Gran moved in with us. And *nobody* felt like doing anything that might take them away from a fan. A breeze would've been a thrill. A *stiff* breeze would've made the front page of the *Daily American Republic*. It was the summer I met Lily, and within five minutes, I was convinced that she was the most horrible girl in the world.

Morningside, being a private drive, saw few travelers. The stately poplars that had once symmetrically flanked its sides were now overgrown and formed a tangled, green canopy, which squeezed out the summer sun, leaving only stale air beneath. We had called it the "Tunnel of Leaves" as far back as any of us could remember because it felt like a portal to somewhere else in time. The south end of Morningside connected to Winding Way, that sinuous loop where everyone who was anyone *had* to live. It was a dull street where nothing ever happened. And the north end of Morningside dumped out right in front of Gran's old house, that unassuming clapboard, where anything was possible.

When Gran wandered off that Tuesday, it was the last straw. She had set off for Uncle Richie's Café to meet Tess and Wilma for lunch, but had never showed up. While Verna Welch was feeding the ducks in the park, she had noticed Gran walking down the middle of Main Street and had dutifully led her safely home.

Dad and I had grown more and more uneasy about letting Gran live alone. Forgetting to feed Percy was one thing; he was a resourceful old puss and if push came to shove, he could look after himself. And forgetting to lock the doors at night didn't warrant a fuss. But when Gran took to wandering off, that was something else again. So with her consent and without fanfare, we piled her lifetime's accumulation of stuff into the back of Dad's ratty, blue pick up and hauled it over to our house.

It was a somber day for all of us.

Doc had built Gran's house as a wedding present, and the day he carried her across its threshold, she vowed she'd never live any place else. I lost count of how many times I'd heard her say, "They're going to have to drag my old bones out."

But after sixty-five years under its sheltering roof, it wasn't Uncle Richie from the volunteer ambulance crew who finally wheeled Gran's carcass out. It was Dad. And he led her, as dignified as possible, by the forearm. She was still *very* much alive, just a bit dehydrated. Dehydrated and *confused*. A tall glass of pink lemonade took care of her dehydration in short order. But as for her confusion, that was an entirely different kettle of fish.

So that summer our dining room became Gran's entire universe and Dad rented her wonderful, old house to complete strangers.

"Ah! Flowerpot, that feels mighty fine," Gran said.

I wrestled the last bobby pin from her bun, letting her hair cascade down around her shoulders. She loved having me brush her hair every night right after the supper dishes were washed. I'd done it nearly every night since I was three.

"School starts in a week," I informed her.

"Is that right?"

"DUN DA DA DUN! This is it Gran. I'm *finally* a senior."

"Is that right? I knew you could do it. You're stubborn as a post."

"Is that your idea of a compliment?" I asked.

"You know what I mean. Sometimes a woman has to be stubborn as a post."

"Well, if it's a compliment, then I s'pose I'd better say thank you," I teased.

"Only a few had the guts to say it to my face. The rest said it behind my back."

"What're ya talkin' about, Gran?"

"They said *I* was stubborn as a post."

"Who said that?" I asked.

"*They* did. They all did."

I didn't have the foggiest idea what she was talking about. It must've been something that happened to her a long time ago. It seemed funny to me that she could remember precisely what happened to her thirty or forty years ago and yet forget how to put on her own dress in the morning.

"It's okay to say *no*. And sometimes…you have to stand up and say *hell no*."

"I know, Gran. You already told me."

"How many times have I already told you?" she asked.

"Too many to count."

"Well…good. I don't want you to ever forget it."

"I won't," I promised.

"You keep at it and I'm fixin' to go to sleep."

"You go right ahead," I said as I worked the brush through her wiry hair.

"I just might. But I'm a might peckish. I'd like a bite of breakfast first."

"Gran?"

"Yes, Flowerpot?"

"You've already eaten your breakfast today."

"Is that right?"

She turned her head to one side so she could see my face. I laughed at how genuinely surprised she looked. She laughed too.

"Yeah, Gran, that's right."

"It has a mind of its own," she remarked.

"What does?"

"My hair. I reckon it gets more ornery each passing year."

"Nah. Your hair is simply beautimus."

"Beautimus," she repeated with a low chuckle. "Flowerpot, you think you'll make a fine hairdresser?"

"Nah. Ya know I haven't wanted to be a hairdresser since I was in the fourth grade. I'm going to be a teacher, just like you used to be."

"A teacher," she mused. I knew she had slipped into pensive mode knitting her brow in fine, crepe wrinkles.

"I'll make out just fine. Ya never need ta worry about me, Gran."

"But I do," she confessed as she looked up at me tenderly. Her eyes were red-rimmed and watery and the lower lids hung down, away from her eyeballs. It hurt me just to look at them.

"Ah! That feels *wonderful*. I haven't had my hair brushed like this in years."

"Gran?"

"Yes, Flowerpot?"

"I brushed your hair last night."

"Is that right?"

Dad was right. Gran *was* getting worse.

Percy lay on Gran's lap, waiting patiently and gazing up at her. As I gently brushed Gran's hair, I watched him and he watched Gran. She wasn't grooming him. Had she forgotten? Could it be possible? Always before, as I brushed her hair, she brushed his, but not tonight. Tonight she just sat. Sat and stared. And he just sat on her lap and waited.

"Gran?" I asked timidly.

"Yes, Flowerpot?"

"Percy's ruff is fluffy, but aren't ya gonna brush his underside tonight?"

She sat quietly for a while and then turned her head so that I could see her face. She looked through me as if I weren't even in the room.

I cringed.

🍁   🍁   🍁

Gran had named the cat Percevel to honor her favorite artist-Norman Rockwell. She always called him Percevel, but she was the only person who ever did. Dad wasn't the sort to waste a single syllable, so he shortened the cat's name to "Percy" and the nickname stuck. Percy was just a hank of fluff when Gran had rescued him from a mile marker by the highway. He was the *biggest* kitten any of us had ever seen.

Gran began to feed him cheese nibblings.

"You're gonna make that cat fat," I teased. "One a these days he's gonna get caught in his kitty door, halfway in and halfway out. His ol' hind end'll be winkin' at the sun, and then where'll he be?"

"No, not Percevel," she said solemnly. "There's not an ounce of fat on him," Gran announced as if she were his own, proud mother.

She picked up Percy's grooming brush and raked it across his backside. After a few more clumsy passes, she lay the brush quietly on the table.

"Did I get it right, Flowerpot?" she asked.

"Yeah, Gran. You got it right."

She smiled up at me.

"C'mon. Let me help ya into bed."

As she was settling, I commenced to tidying up the place. She had left behind a bedroom papered with cabbage roses to settle into this tired, old dining room with walls of mover's beige. It wasn't a fair trade. I leaned over her small form and studied her face carefully.

She cleared her throat once or twice and rubbed her two paper-thin lips together.

"Do you think they'll find my baby?"

"Sure they will," I answered using my most reassuring voice and I gave her hand a little squeeze. Then I patted the foot of her bed-Percy's signal to retire.

He was fifteen years old and nearly blind, so he no longer bounded onto the bed, but instead carefully *felt* his way up the old quilt.

🍁 🍁 🍁

"Good mornin', Gran," I called out.

If she heard me, she didn't let on, slumped over in her old rocking chair, oblivious to the world. I peeled the fusty, urine-soaked sheets from her bed, rolled them into a soft, large ball and deposited them into the washing machine. After I sanitized her mattress and let it air dry, I fitted it with clean sheets.

Now she was rocking back and forth with Percy bunched up on her lap.

"I'm sorry about the mess, Flowerpot."

"Ah! It's nothin'."

She smiled at me.

And I smiled back.

I couldn't help wondering if she even realized that strangers had moved into her house. I smoothed the ripples out of the quilt.

"You hungry, Percy?"

He slid effortlessly off Gran's lap and headed for the kitchen.

"NOW!" he bellowed and I obediently dumped a can of "Tasty Liver Dinner" into his bowl.

I grabbed some pastrami from the fridge. (I loved meat sandwiches for breakfast and cereal for supper.)

"That meat's loud, Flowerpot. Better not eat it. It'll throw yer whole body outta kilter. Now go on out and fetch the mail," Dad ordered.

🍁 🍁 🍁

He always stood by the trash can when he went through the morning mail–an economy of motion, as most of the day's haul went straight in.

"Gah! Looks like ol' Percy here's got another one of them pre-approved credit cards."

He ripped the envelope open, unfolded the crisp, white letter, and read the message loudly enough for Gran to hear in the dining room.

> "PERCEVEL TAIT,
> A CREDIT RATING LIKE YOURS DESERVES TO BE REWARDED."

He let his arm hang limp and dangled the letter tantalizingly.

"Here, Percy!"

In an instant eighteen pounds of Maine Coon thumped across the linoleum floor. Percy gave the letter a good, hard sniffing and convinced that it was neither edible nor dangerous, clamped it in his chops and carried it away.

"What kind of bank would send a cat a credit card?" he muttered to himself as he finished the last of his morning coffee. "Just plain stoogey."

🍁 🍁 🍁

Only ten-thirty in the morning and it was already so hot that Healy Street seemed to waver in the sun, mirage-like. Since the soles of my shoes were sticking to the asphalt, I reckoned we were in for another scorcher. I had made up my mind the night before to pay the strangers a little visit. After all, I had waited an entire week and that should be long enough for *anybody* to get moved in. How much stuff could two people have?

Except for Lawrence Winslow's old basset hound that slept in the middle of the road, Main Street was deserted. As soon as I turned down Winding Way, I was doused with the smell of freshly cut grass. I s'pose it was smart to get all of the outside chores squared away first thing in the morning, before the heat settled in and drove everyone in front of a fan. (Or an air conditioner, if you were lucky enough to afford it.) I was relieved to turn onto Morningside. The tunnel of leaves was a welcome respite from the oppressive heat. Those old poplars must've shaved off ten whole degrees.

Near the end of the tunnel of leaves, yellow clapboards and brown shingles peeked from behind the sloppy branches. Gran's place looked like an oversized doll's house that had been plopped smack in the middle of a dusty lot. It seemed pitifully bare without the dazzling beds of zinnias and marigolds. This was the first year she hadn't planted a flower garden out front. I stepped from under the protection of the poplars, squinted my blue eyes from the brutal sun, and ran my fingers like a makeshift comb through my blond hair. I followed the cobblestone walk around the enormous bow window that jutted out in front.

It looked like I wasn't the only one who hadn't gotten used to the idea of strangers living in Gran's house. Percy was already on his morning patrol, standing vigil when I arrived. He had started stalking something beside the front porch, so I kicked a dirt clod and sent it flying. I wanted to give whatever poor creature he had cornered a sporting chance. (Although Percy was old and nearly blind, he remained an excellent mouser.) He turned quickly, raised and lowered his head as if to acknowledge my presence, and continued the hunt.

With him there for moral support, I sucked in a long, steadying breath, climbed the two front steps, and pounded on the screen door.

An extremely tall woman soon peered out.

"Yes?"

"Uh. Hello. My name is Senga and um...I just came by to welcome you...uh...welcome you to the neighborhood." (I hoped my smile didn't look half as fake as it felt.)

"How thoughtful," the woman said. "Senga. What a lovely name."

"Thank you," I replied. That's when I was struck with the sudden thought that I should've brought a housewarming gift, like a basket of muffins or something.

"So, what grade are you in, Senga?"

But before I could even answer, a younger, browner version of the woman suddenly appeared beside her in the open doorway. I blinked hard. Amazons! I'd read about them *and* seen photographs of them in the nature magazines, but until now had never seen one in real life. They stepped out onto the front porch. Standing at least six feet tall, they seemed to tower over me and I suddenly felt very small and inadequate.

"Huh?" I mumbled.

"What grade are you in, Senga?" the woman repeated.

"Senior. I mean...this year I'll be a senior...in the twelfth grade."

The woman turned to the girl and said, "It looks like you've met your first classmate."

I thought the girl couldn't possibly have been my age, not unless she'd flunked -a couple of times.

She narrowed her eyes and studied me. Starting with my face and taking her time, she seemed to be inspecting me, from my face all the way down to my tennis shoes and then back up again. When she finished, she flared her nostrils and sniffed. Then she turned toward the woman as if I were completely irrelevant and dismissible.

But I continued to look at her. And I got that same feeling I always had whenever I stood too close to the porcelain dolls on display at The Carriage House. I recalled the sign that hung prominently above them in their case:

YOU BREAK IT,
YOU BOUGHT IT.

There was no doubt about it: the girl was exquisite. She brushed a loose strand of long, black hair from her right eye.

It was the woman who finally broke the awkward silence.

"I'm Janelle and this is Lily."

I thrust my hand toward Janelle and she shook it warmly. I offered my hand to Lily but she stood stock-still and regarded me the way a sympathetic nurse might a very ill child.

"She doesn't shake hands," Janelle explained.

"Oh!" I heard myself say quite unexpectedly and retracted my outstretched hand. (Gee. I'd never met anybody who didn't shake hands.)

"Well…It looks like you're making yourselves right at home," I said, nervously shifting my weight from foot to foot.

"Ri-ight," Lily said as if it were two, separate words. "The wallpaper is ridiculously old fashioned. I'll have to rip it all off the walls and paint them a decent color." She brandished a hand-held vacuum above her head like an impromptu weapon as she continued to talk. "And hairballs seem to magically appear right out of the woodwork, but I suppose…it won't be half-bad…once we get the old people smell out of the house."

Heat rushed my face and bulged at both temples. My hands balled into fists. (The last time that happened, I broke Leroy's nose for calling my aunt Gladys a "retard.") If Janelle hadn't been standing there, I certainly would've broken Lily's nose. I had to get a grip on myself.

So I trained my eyes on Janelle. "If you need somethin', I'm right off Main. Only blue house on Healy."

I stepped off the porch, imagining Lily's gimlet eyes boring holes into my back and I headed down Morningside. Under the protection of those prolific poplars, I removed my glasses and wiped away stinging tears.

September

I didn't see Lily again until school started. Right before the morning assembly, she singled me out and stuck to my side like a burr. Maybe it was because I had made that awkward attempt to welcome her and Janelle to the neighborhood, or maybe it was because she still didn't know anyone else her age in town. Either way, I didn't care. She was at the top of everyone's gossip list, and here she was-sitting next to me! (And I *wasn't* one of the popular girls.)

Apparently she hadn't held it against me that I'd neglected to bring them a housewarming gift, so I decided to let that crack about the "old people smell" go unpunished. After all, *everyone* says something stupid once in a while. It's what separates us from the animals. And I wasn't the sort to carry a grudge.

🍁   🍁   🍁

"Lemme see your schedule."
Lily unfolded the computer printout and handed it to me.
"Do we have any classes together?" she asked.
"Yeah, almost every one. Now what're the odds of that?"

❦   ❦   ❦

If I could change only one thing about high school, I'd made the breaks between classes longer. And not to squander the newfound time standing on "the hill" smoking cigarettes with the wilder guys. I just hate to be rushed.

I'd quickly discovered that Lily was a good person to know between classes. She was noticeably taller than every girl (and an embarrassing number of guys) in school and could expertly maneuver the two of us through the hallway crush. Stung by a few of her razor-sharp barbs, underclassmen withered and we walked through them all like Lily had just parted the Red Sea.

"Step aside, Bosephus!" Lily whiplashed. The freckled sophomore nearly leapt out of her way.

In the bathroom, I asked, "Lily, do you have to be so *mean*?"

"Mean?" she repeated.

"Abrasive," I clarified.

"Abrasive?" she repeated.

"It's beginnin' ta sound like an echo chamber in here," I said.

"Look, Senga, I've been jettisoned into Swamp East and have befriended their queen. This is as *nice* as I'm going to get."

I bristled.

"So…how'd ya manage ta wind up livin' here? I mean…ya got family around these parts?"

"Just the luck of the draw," she answered as she reapplied her lipstick.

I made a decision about Lily right then and there. We were just *too* different. For instance, Lily carried a complete, but miniature makeup kit in her hand-tooled leather bag. I didn't even carry a comb. And Lily studied her image in the mirror after *every* class-almost as if she'd forgotten what she looked like. I glanced at myself once in the morning, as I bolted out of my house. She was supermodel thin. I was…well, I wasn't.

"Do you think I'm fat?" I asked.

"Why? Do *you* think you're fat?"

"Well," I began, grabbing a soft roll of midriff, "I s'pose I *am* doughy around the middle. But Gran says I'm not fat, I'm just a girl that likes her food. She says I have a *healthy appetite*."

"Well, then…If that's what your Gran said…then you go right on believing it."

Lily suddenly stopped preening. Then she carefully folded and stowed her compact hairbrush. She turned her head slightly and stared hard at my reflection in the mirror.

I grew more and more uncomfortable under her scrutiny.

"What?" I asked uneasily.

"How'd *you* ever get a name like Senga?"

"My mom and Gran named me."

"Is it Indian?"

"Nah."

"Japanese?"

"Nah. My mom's name was Agnes. So's my gran's. They both really wanted to name me Little Agnes."

"Lucky you," Lily quipped.

I pretended to ignore her remark.

"Anywho, they decided against it; three Agnes's would be too much of a good thing. So they spelled AGNES backwards and came up with SENGA."

"That was clever," Lily said.

I was never completely sure if she was being serious or sarcastic.

"Do you think my name makes me sound like I'm oriental?"

"*News flash!* Two things are oriental-food and rugs. People are Asian."

"Oh! I didn't mean nothin' by it."

"I'm sure you didn't," Lily said.

She continued to study my reflection in the mirror. "I've been to seven different schools so far and if there's one thing I've learned it's that it pays to watch what you say."

I nodded.

"I think we should switch names. Don't you?"

"Whaddya mean?"

"My name suits you to a tee, with your pasty skin and white-blond hair, but I've never really felt it *fit* me. But Senga…now that's an exotic name…That's a name I could really do something with. It rolls off my tongue like music or like I'm casting a spell."

Now I'd never considered my name to sound the least bit magical. To me it had always been just Agnes spelled backwards.

"Do you smoke?" Lily asked abruptly.

I was afraid she might light up, right then and there in the girls' bathroom and the last thing I needed was a detention.

"Nah."

"Well, that's a relief. I absolutely *hate* the way cigarette smoke clings to my hair. It's positively nasty."

There is *one* girl and perhaps a handful of guys in every school who leave the distinct impression that they're direct descendents of criminals. They are the kind of human beings who would hang a puppy just because they could get away with it. At our high school, Red had that role completely sewed up. She was the nucleus of a herd of dull, ugly girls. I couldn't vouch for all of them, but I was convinced that Trish and Jazz, her two closest minions, weren't genuinely evil girls, they were just too insecure to stand up to Red. And I was careful not to judge them too harshly; Red could be beastly. I caught a glimpse of the trio as they entered the bathroom. And I shuddered as they gathered around Lily and me like a storm.

Red glared at us, but said nothing. In less than a minute, the threatening trio disappeared. I guess she had just wanted her presence to be felt.

"Ugh! What *was* that smell?" Lily demanded with her nose crinkled, rabbit-like.

"We *are* in the bathroom," I answered.

She rolled her soft, brown eyes at me.

"Didn't you smell it?"

"Nah. I didn't smell anything."

She leaned close and giggled, "It must've been Red's cologne. They don't call it toilet water for nothing."

I didn't even crack a smile. "Lily, you'd better not mess with Red and her girls. All it would take is a wink or a sneer and they'd light on you like flies on a dead dog."

"Big deal," she said flatly. "There was *no way* she could've heard me."

"Maybe these walls have ears. Ya never know," I countered.

She eyed me suspiciously.

"I'm not messin' around. I'm dead serious, Lily. Red's dad is the sheriff."

"Well…that's straight from the book *Who Cares?*"

"He's an important man around here."

"Ooh! Look at me, Senga. I'm shaking."

"If she wanted to, she could make your life unbearable."

"It's easy to look like a big frog when you're sitting in a small pond," Lily answered as she ran a delicate, gold comb through her glassy smooth hair.

We were just too different.

Lily *wasn't* like me at all.

She was fearless.

❦   ❦   ❦

"You have the prettiest black hair," I admired aloud.

"It's not black."
"What're you talkin' about?"
"It's *light* black."
"Uh...Light black would be gray."
She quickly changed the subject.
"Have you ever thought of getting braces?"

I wanted to say, "Yeah, every single time I look in the mirror." But I didn't say anything. I just shrugged.

"I don't know the first thing about Guatemala," she complained.
"Honduras," I corrected.
"Whatever."

Lily depressed the lever on the paper towel dispenser three times and let the paper hang freely as she scrubbed at the ink stain on her middle finger. When she was satisfied with her cleaning effort, she rinsed all of the soap from her hands, tore off the paper towel, dried her hands, and then used it to turn off the spigot. I'd never seen anyone do it that way before and I was impressed. I would've just used my clean hands to turn off the dirty tap and my hands would've been all germy again.

But Lily managed to keep her hands clean.

"I already checked out a book on Central America. And since we only have to write one page on Honduras, how hard could it be?"

"How would you like to come over after school so we can work on it together?"

"Are you sure your mother won't mind?" I asked.
"Who? Janelle?"
"Yeah."
"She won't mind."

"Ya know...You're the only person I ever met who calls her mother by her first name."

"Janelle's not my mother," Lily said matter-of-factly.
"Well, you look *just* like her. I just thought..."
"Well, you were wrong," Lily said.

I *knew* they looked alike, but why argue over something that didn't amount to a hill of beans?

"Then why do you live with her?" I pressed.

"She's my legal guardian," Lily snapped, looking annoyed that I'd dared to ask her anything so personal. "She adopted me when my parents were killed, okay?"

"I'm really sorry," I offered.

"No big deal. They must've met in college or something 'cause Janelle told me that she'd known my dad forever."

"Is she nice?"

"Who?"

"Janelle. She seems real nice."

"Yes, she's nice. And she's more like a big sister than a mother. That has certain ad-van-tag-es. (The way she pronounced it made me wonder what these advantages might be.)

"C'mon. We're gonna be late for class," I urged.

"Get the door for me, will you?" Lily asked.

"Sure."

I'd never known anyone like Lily before. She was so pulled together and self-assured. If tomorrow morning she would've showed up at school wearing one of those cheesy fake fur toilet covers, the rest of us would just have to admit, "Aha! So *that's* what we should be wearing this year."

The rest of the school day dragged. By 3:05, I was already at the flagpole waiting for Lily. With a sideward glance, I caught Harrison trying to sneak up behind me. He covered both of my eyes with his broad hand.

"Guess who?"

"Hey, Harrison."

"I just wanted to tell you somethin'. Got a minute?"

"Sure."

"I don't think it's such a hot idea for you to be hangin' around with that new girl," he said.

"Who? Lily? And why's that?"

"You been under some rock? Everyone's talkin' 'bout how half the football team's seen her undress in front of her bedroom window. And from what I hear…she puts on a pretty good show."

I bashed him in the chest, but he grabbed my hand playfully.

"I'm not kiddin', Senga," He said seriously.

"Well, shame on them! What the devil were they doin' all the way down Morningside Drive? I have half a mind to tell Lily so that she can have the whole lot of 'em arrested. That *is* private property, you know."

"Aw! Don't get sore, Senga. I just wouldn't want you to hang around with someone who might tarnish your reputation. Remember, I'm gonna marry you one of these days." (He had had a crush on me since the second grade.)

"How could I possibly forget? You've told me nearly every day for the past ten years."

"Here she comes now. I gotta go. Don't say nothin' to her 'bout it."

He left as quickly and as unobtrusively as a six-foot, two-inch boy could.

"Hey, Lily!"

"How'd you get here so fast?" she asked.

"Pack right, travel light."

"What did you just say?"

"Ah, never mind. It was just somethin' Gran used to say all of the time."

"O-kay."

"You still wanna work together at your house?"

"Of course I do."

"Well, I'll have to swing by my house first to let Dad know what I'm doin'. He gets all hot and bothered if he doesn't know where I am and what I'm up to."

We walked down Healy without saying a word.

"Do you have any brothers or sisters?" I finally asked-more to break the silence than anything else.

"Have you seen any?"

I shook my head no.

"I'm an only. How about you?"

"I have three older brothers," I said.

"Sheesh, your parents must be really old."

"It's just my dad. I reckon he is. It's just not somethin' I go around thinkin' about."

"And your mother?"

"She passed away."

"Passed away. Hey! I like a good euphemism myself," Lily smiled.

My face must have looked blank, because Lily jumped into an explanation.

"A euphemism is what you have when you substitute a pleasant expression for a blunt one. You said, 'passed away' when you could just as easily have said, 'croaked'."

I tried to change the subject.

"Didja know that I'm what Gran calls a *change of life* baby?"

"And why is that?"

"I reckon because when I was born, it changed everybody's life."

Lily didn't laugh.

"I was a big surprise to everybody. Gran told me that my mother had already gone through the change-or at least she thought she had-when she found out she was pregnant with me."

But Lily would not be sidetracked.

"So, how'd your mother die?"

"Somethin' was wrong with her heart. Dad said she died fast, didn't suffer much."

"I suppose if you have to die, that would be the way to do it, not suffering much."

"So, where're you from exactly?" I hazarded since she had felt so free to delve into my business.

"Why? Don't I look *American* enough for you?"

I couldn't tell whether or not she was teasing.

"Of course," I said.

"Well…My dad was American, from Billerica, outside Boston. He was in the Air Force stationed in Manila when he met and married my mother. She was *beautiful*. I have a photograph of her at home I'll show you. She was considered quite tall for a Filipino."

"How about your dad? Was he tall?"

"He was a very tall man-six feet, six inches."

"That *is* tall," I said. "I reckon that explains how you come to be so tall. What are you? Six feet?"

"I'm five twelve," she said with a sweet conspiring smile.

"It musta been wonderful to travel around the way you have."

"It was okay," Lily said.

"Where's the neatest place you've ever been?"

"Lived? Or just visited?" She asked.

"Lived."

"Hands down, Honolulu, Hawaii."

"It's easy to see why," I said. "Not that I've ever been there or anything. But 'cause of the beautiful weather."

"Well, of course the weather is beautiful. You'll get no argument from me. But that's not why. I loved it there because I felt like I really *fit in*. Seems like *everyone* there was of mixed race-light brown and beautiful."

"It sounds awesome."

"I even learned a little pigeon while I was there."

"Pigeon?" I asked.

"You know…the vernacular of the common people."

"The what?"

"What Yiddish is to German Jews, Pigeon is to Hawaiian islanders."

"Oh! Well…then…how about the worst place you've ever lived?"

"Sacramento, California. Definitely."

"Yeah? And why's that?"

"The air. It was just plain nasty. The farmers used to burn their rice fields every year and it just about drove my sinuses crazy! Thanks to that assignment, I have chronic diseased mucosa of the left maxillary sinus."

"That can't be good," I said.

She let out a tired laugh. "No, Senga, it can't be good."

"Where else have you lived?"

"Let's see…I've spent most of my summers in Seattle with Janelle's friends. And we always take the ferry up to Victoria."

"Victoria?"

"British Columbia."

I didn't say anything.

"You know…Canada?"

"Yeah, sure."

"Then I lived in Florida…and England…and southern California…which is just as nasty as northern California, but for an entirely different reason."

"Any place else?"

"Janelle got an assignment to Minot Air Force Base, North Dakota."

"Didja like it there?"

"It was okay. We didn't live on base long. Janelle rented a house in a little town near the base and we lived there. "

"Wouldja ever wanna move back there?"

"No way."

"Why not?" I asked.

"For a couple of reasons. First of all, everything you've ever heard about winters in North Dakota is true."

"I haven't heard anything about the winters in North Dakota. Come to think of it, I haven't heard anything about *anything* in North Dakota."

"There's a reason for that."

"But I *did* see *Fargo*. Does that count?"

Lily rolled her marvelous brown eyes.

"Winters are as cold as a witch's tit. Sheesh! Once that wind came screaming across the prairie, driving that mercury down, I thought it would rip the skin right off my face. It was brutal. You have *never* felt cold like that, Senga. And, believe me, you never want to."

I nodded in agreement. It sounded hideous.

"What else?" I asked. "You said you had a couple a reasons. Couple means two, last time I checked."

"Oh, yeah. It's the only place I've ever lived where somebody stole something right out of our front yard! Some idiot stole Janelle's cat statue. It had been safely buried in snow all winter, but with the spring thaw, we saw first one ear and then the other. Soon the little face was sitting on top of a mound of dirty snow and then one day…the statue was gone."

"Why is that so unusual? There's thieves anyplace you're likely to go."

"I know that. And it wasn't…the money so much either. That little statue only cost $39.95. It was the *principle* of the thing. Janelle had that cat statue for years and years and nobody had *ever* laid a finger on it. And we'd lived in some pretty rough neighborhoods from time to time. We'd taken it with us from house to house whenever we moved. Then we move to North Dakota and PRESTO someone lifts it right out of our front yard! It still makes my blood boil every time I think about it."

"Maybe you could find another one."

"You mean in somebody's yard?"

"Ha! Nah, I didn't mean that. I meant that maybe you might be lucky enough to find one at a store one of these days."

"Maybe."

"Is that why you left North Dakota?"

"No. We left because Janelle couldn't find a decent job. Just think…a nurse with a Master's degree and twenty years of military experience and nobody would hire her. I couldn't bear to see her self esteem drop through the floor, so I nagged at her till she got this job."

"Oh! I wondered how you wound up in this town."

"Have you ever seen a grownup cry?"

I had to stop and think for a minute. Had I?

"Nah, I don't reckon I ever have."

"Well…believe me…you don't *want* to. Getting Janelle out of that situation was the best thing we could've ever done."

"All things considered…I would still hafta say that I'm jealous of all the travelin' around you've done, all the people you've met…all the places you've seen."

"I suppose you are."

I knew Lily didn't mean it the way it sounded.

"We've traveled just about everywhere," she added. "Janelle had plum assignments all the way through her military career and every time she took leave, she'd drag me all over the place looking for her little bits of junk."

"Oh! I didn't know Janelle was a collector."

"Ha! That's a good one, Senga!" Lily said as she threw her head back in laughter.

I didn't have the foggiest idea why she was laughing.

"What is *collector* a euphemism for?" Lily asked.

"I dunno. What is *collector* a euphemism for? I have no idea."

"A PACK RAT!" Lily answered. "I'll have to tell this one to Janelle."

All that talk about travel had lowered my mood a few pegs.

"I can't wait ta get out of here," I said.

"Why is that? This place seems to be just as good as any. I think it would be wonderful to live in a small town like this all the way through school. Just think…you'd know everybody and everybody would know you. Has this town always been this size?"

"Pretty much. Gran told me that the population sign at the city limits hasn't ever been changed; every time some girl gets pregnant, some guy leaves town."

"I have a good feeling about this place."

"I reckon it's okay. I don't really have any place to compare it to, 'cause I've never been anyplace else."

Lily's eyes narrowed to slits.

"You have *got* to be kidding."

Embarrassed, I shook my head no.

"Well, we will just have to remedy that," she said as her left eyebrow arched mysteriously.

"It's not that easy, Lily."

"Sure it is."

"Nah. I could never leave Gran."

※　　　※　　　※

I introduced Lily to Dad that afternoon. And for the first time in a long time, maybe the first time ever, I took a good, hard look at the place I called home. Lily probably wouldn't want to hang around with me once she got a good look at my house and realized I didn't have two nickels to scrape together. And who could blame her?

She was very polite to Dad. I could tell that he was impressed with her. I would've introduced Lily to Gran that afternoon as well, but Dad told me it would be better if I didn't. Gran had good days and bad days. And this week…the scales had tipped in favor of the bad.

❦ ❦ ❦

We didn't say more than two words to each other all the way to Lily's. What was she thinking? Was she mentally trying out the right set of words to dump me gently?

Lily unlocked her front door. She took off her shoes in the vestibule, so I did the same. (Lily said *everybody* did that in Hawaii.) I half expected to see a house filled to overflowing with the rewards of being a packrat; I'd been in houses before where every nook and cranny was bursting, stuffed to the gills with treasures that couldn't be stowed or parted with. I'd been in living rooms that resembled low, rolling hills, which were actually just mounds of stuff that took on a life of their own.

I was surprised to see how orderly everything was. I reckoned Janelle was a very discriminating packrat.

I followed Lily into the living room and we plopped our backpacks on the living room floor.

"So, is your dad some great cook?" she asked.

"I've never had ptomaine, if that's what you're askin'. He's alright, I guess."

"He sure looked saucy in that apron," Lily said with a sly smile.

Ewww. The thought...

"Sometimes I think he's way too involved with that crockpot."

"Well, I think it's sweet that he cooks and cleans and tries to take care of you," Lily said. "I mean, that's just something you don't see every day of the week."

"Don't give him too much credit. It was really Gran who raised me. I reckon I spent more time in this house than I ever spent in mine."

"What are you talking about? *This* house."

"*This* house," I answered as I patted the soft, worn carpet. "I thought you knew."

"*Knew?*"

"This is Gran's house. Janelle is renting it from Dad."

It took a few seconds for Lily to process this vital bit of information and I could almost see the gears grinding in her head.

"Sheesh!"

"Do you remember that day I came over…that first day I ever met you?"

"Of course I remember."

"And you made that remark about getting the 'old people smell' out?"

She nodded.

"You didn't know how close you came to getting your nose mashed."

But Lily didn't apologize.

🍁 🍁 🍁

"Come upstairs. I want to show you something."

I followed her up the familiar staircase and into her bedroom. It used to be *my* bedroom when I stayed with Gran. Lily pulled out an enormous burgundy leather photo album and proudly set it on my lap.

"What's this?" I asked.

"This…is my passion. Go ahead, Senga. You can open it."

So I carefully opened the cover. Page after page, I carefully turned and looked at each photograph while Lily stood close behind me, peering over my shoulder. As hard as I tried, I couldn't understand what I was supposed to be admiring.

If I didn't know better I would've thought I might be in one of those Candid Camera segments where everyone else is in on the joke and you're left out, looking like some fool.

"What are they?" I finally broke down and forced myself to ask.

"They're scratches," Lily explained.

"*Scratches?*" I asked incredulously. "You take *pictures* of *scratches*?"

"Of course," she answered—as if photographing scratches was the most ordinary thing in the world.

"Janelle and I knew the best stevedores on Oahu and they let us lurk around and photograph any damage on the Matson containers. Janelle's album isn't nearly as breathtaking as mine, but she tries so hard."

I wasn't going to tell her that I didn't have a clue as to what a stevedore was. But I made a mental note to look it up in my dictionary just as soon as I got home that evening. I leafed through each page…again…this time slowly.

Although I hated to admit it, the scratches were beautiful.

🍁 🍁 🍁

"Have you ever really *mashed* someone's nose, Senga?" Lily asked curiously.

"Oh! Hell yeah. Leroy Webster called my aunt Gladys a 'retard' and I let him have it."

"*Was* she a retard?"

"Yeah, but that wasn't the point. Leroy had absolutely no business calling her one. Especially when I was within earshot."

October

The smell of rotting fish announced Palmer Slough long before we could see it or hear its tired ripples lick the dock's legs. Percy led the way. He picked his way on padded paws across the rocks until he reached the highest one and then nosed rudely into a clump of squat, brown mushrooms, mowing them down. Their pithy, wet stalks snapped flush with the crevice lip that had been their cradle. Sluggishly, he draped his solid body over the hot rock and soaked the remnant warmth into his old, feline bones.

"Why do you bother coming to this stink hole?" Lily demanded.

"I dunno. I can't really explain it. I just feel…kinda…peaceful here."

"What's *country club* a euphemism for?" Lily asked.

"I dunno."

"You're not even *trying*!" she wailed.

"Well, I give up. What is *country club* a euphemism for?"

"A country club is an outhouse with *two* seats."

"Ha! I actually liked that one," I said.

Lily was pleased with herself. I knew because she flashed her flawless smile.

"Do you believe in guardian angels?" she asked.

"Isn't that a Catholic thing?"

"Maybe," she shrugged.

"Are you Catholic?"

"Yes. Aren't you?'" Lily raised a suspicious brow.
"Nah. Baptist."
"Well, *do* you?"
"Do I what?"
"Do you believe in guardian angels?" Lily repeated.
"I reckon I might."

I skipped a stone across the slough. Skip…skip…skip…skip…plop.

"You're pretty good at that," Lily said.
"It ain't hard. Here. Give it a try," I urged as I handed her a smooth stone that I had picked up.
"Ploop!"

The stone sank in the middle of expanding, concentric rings.
"It takes some gettin' used to."
"I guess so."
"Why'dja ask me about guardian angels? Do *you* believe in them?"
"Yes. At least…I've often had the feeling…that someone…or something was always watching over me," Lily confessed.

Lily looked beautiful standing there, with the October sunlight gleaming off her sleek, *light* black hair. And for a minute, I almost wished I were Catholic so that I could have my own guardian angel.

"What is *wrong* with that cat?" Lily demanded.

Percy's whiskers and front paws were twitching rapidly.
"Is he having a seizure?"

I glanced his way.
"Nah. He's just dreamin'."
"Cats dream?" Lily's disbelief was palpable.
"Sure they do," I answered matter-of-factly.
"Who told you that?"
"Gran."

Lily lowered her head so that she had to roll her eyeballs up severely in order to see me. "Senga, your gran thinks you are a flowerpot, so why in the world would you believe her when she told you that cats dream?"

Her condescending tone cut to the quick.

"Gran doesn't think I'm a flowerpot, Lily. It's just my nickname. I know it's a *stupid* nickname, but that's what everybody in my family calls me. If Gran said cats dream, then you could bet the farm she's right."

"Did your gran ever bother to tell you what cats dream about?"

"The usual stuff-cheese nibblin's, saucers of thick cream, mouse heads."

Lily winced.

"You ought to see him when his paws really get goin'. Gran said he's most likely dreamin' of way back when. Maybe when he was just a kitten, scurryin' up some old tree."

"Well, I wouldn't know anything about that. I'm looking at him right now and it looks like he's having a nightmare. Shouldn't we wake him? Poke him with a stick or something?"

"Nah. Don't rankle him."

As we watched, Percy suddenly stopped his twitching and stood bolt upright. He sprang into action as surely as if someone had flipped a little switch hidden in his fur. With nose alert and whiskers ready, Percy stealthily stalked around a bunch of sticker bushes by the water's edge.

"What is he doing now?" Lily wondered out loud.

"He musta caught wind of somethin'."

We sneaked behind him toward the bushes.

"Lily, be careful. I've seen cottonmouths down here and they're real mean snakes."

"There's something under there," Lily said as she pushed back some of the scraggly branches. She tugged at a tangled fishing line with a pair of men's briefs tied to one end. "Ewwww! Wonder what they were trying to catch?"

She tossed it back. Then she pulled out a dirty, wet pillowcase and peered inside.

"Perfectly vile," she erupted and thrust the soiled pillowcase at me.

Now I'm not the squeamish type. With a dad, three older brothers, and Cousin Duane, Lord knows I've baited hooks galore and gutted my share of fish. But I was completely caught off guard by what I saw at the bottom of that nasty pillowcase.

"Gah! Who would've done something like this?"

I turned away from Lily and puked.

"What're we gonna do with 'em?" I asked.

"Just fling them back under those bushes," Lily responded flatly.

I hated her for saying that.

It took me a minute or so, but I came up with an idea.

"Cmon, we gotta go."

We took the quickest route-down Winding Way and up Main. A stranger wearing an old BDU jacket was lugging his meager belongings into one of the studio apartments beside Uncle Richie's Café. (I assumed he was just another pair of strong hands to help with the harvest. I couldn't have been more wrong.)

Directly behind the studio apartments lived Verna Welch, the town magnet for strays. She shared her rambling, rabbit warren of a house with two dogs, two parakeets, too many cats to count, and ten thousand fleas. If *anybody* could help the pitiful creatures clinging to life at the bottom of this pillowcase, then she was the pony I'd place all bets on.

In no time, we were on Verna's back porch, pounding on her broken screen door.

Verna waddled out.

"Thenga!" she exclaimed with her pronounced lisp. "I haven't theen you in a coon'th age. How'th your gran making do? Eh heh heh heh."

"Oh! She's just fine, Verna. And I wanted to thank you... again...for bringing her home that last time she wandered off."

"I wath jutht glad to be of thervith. The poor thing…thee had thet out to go to the café and forgot where thee wath. When I thaw her, thee wath walking down Main Thtreet, crying to beat the band. It broke my old heart, Thenga. I never thaw a wilder look on a human fathe! It mutht be…downright horrible to loothe your memorieth that way."

"Well, Dad keeps an eagle eye on her now that she's moved in with us."

"Thank the good Lord above. That ith good newth."

I smiled.

Verna turned toward Lily.

"And who might you be? Eh heh heh heh."

"Verna, I'd like you to meet Lily. She's a friend of mine."

"Well, how'dya do?" Verna asked as she extended her plump hand to shake Lily's.

Lily stood motionless-like a six-foot bronze statue erected smack in the middle of Verna's kitchenette.

"Uh! She doesn't shake hands," I heard myself explain.

"Well…I'll be," Verna mumbled under her breath.

"Verna, Percy found these kittens at the slough. Do you think you might be able to do anything?"

I surrendered the wet pillowcase and its sad stowaways to her eager grasp.

"Let me have a little look. Eh heh heh heh."

She carefully opened the pillowcase and when she peered inside, her sweet face puckered as if she were going to bawl.

"Lord thave me!" she wailed.

Her small eyes examined each cold little body as she laid it out on a spread newspaper. The kittens looked mashed. Almost as if the entire pillowcase had been swung round and round with great speed and then slammed against a concrete wall. When she scooped up the last tiny body, a reluctant smile stole over her ample face.

"C'mon, little fella. Don't throw in the towel." Her forehead wrinkled as her lips pursed. "He'th too little...He really ought to be nurthing, but damnathon! Thorry about the thwear word."

"It's okay, Verna," I assured her.

"I don't have any little bottleth around here. Thenga, do you have any tiny bottleth at home? Eh heh heh heh."

Over the years, Verna had learned to soften every request with a nervous giggle. She had grown accustomed to being ignored, laughed at behind her back, and never taken seriously.

"No, I'm afraid I don't have anything like that around my house."

Instinctively, she snatched a dollop of slimy cat food from a nearby dish and sat it on a margarine lid. Then she shoved the skittish visitor so close to the wet mound that his nose nearly poked in. He mewed and with great effort of will, cocked his oversized head to one side.

"Who would've done something like this?" I asked.

No one answered.

"C'mon little fella. Nibble a tiny bit...for Auntie Verna," she pleaded.

She tenderly mashed the kittens two front paws into the slimy cat food. He sniffed at it. He sniffed again. His sandpaper tongue shot out and he tentatively tasted between his toes. When the food was all gone, and his furry little paws had been licked scrupulously clean, he reared back and stared hard at us-first at Verna, then at me. I caught a glimpse of mischief in his pale, blue eyes.

Verna cuddled him in her stained apron. With her free hand, she returned the lifeless little bodies-one by one-to the pillowcase and deposited it into the galvanized bin by her back door.

"Don't worry, Thenga. Eh heh heh heh. They won't be in there long. Only 'til I can dig five little graveth."

"Who is this?" Lily asked.

She held up a pewter frame enclosing the photograph of a beautiful young woman. Lily hadn't paid one bit of attention to the kitten the entire time. Instead, she had been eyeballing everything in Verna's cluttered kitchenette.

"Why...That'th me...when I wath a young girl."

(If that *really* was her in the photograph, then time had been merciless.)

"Verna, how'dja know it would work?" I asked.

"Eathy, Thenga. Catth are meticulouthly clean animalth."

"So...?"

"Well, I *knew* that he would muthter hith latht drop of thtrength to groom himthelf."

"But...How'dja *know*?"

"Thenga, I'm really thurprithed at you! And you been knowin' Perthy all a fifteen yearth...There ith NO WAY any thelf-rethpecting feline would croth over to the other thide looking thlovenly."

She lowered her voice to just above a whisper and added, "Catth have never forgotten that they were wonthe worthiped ath godth, you know."

What could I say to that?

Verna leaned so close that I could smell the onions she'd had for lunch.

"Haven't you ever wondered what they talk about...late at night...with all their off-key caterwauling? Eh heh heh heh."

I wanted to laugh out loud. And I would've too, if Verna hadn't looked so darn serious.

"And he *wath* at the very bottom of the pillowcathe. Hith brotherth' and thithterth' little bodieth had buffered him and kept him warm," she confided.

"Thank you, Verna...I really wouldn't have known what to do on my own. He wouldn't've made it."

Her fleshy face broke out in a brilliant smile.

I glanced at Lily.

She looked awfully bored.

"Aha!" Verna snorted. "I almotht forgot to tell you. Perthy paid me a little vithit a while back."

"Did he?"

Nothing Percy did managed to surprise me anymore.

"He bringth me little prethenth now and again."

"I didn't know."

Verna continued, "Yeth, he brought me a dead mouthe. He meowed fit to be tied at the back door until I came out. I guethth he wanted me to know the mouthe wath from him. He'th quite a gentleman that way, you know."

I've never thought of Percy as a gentleman, but I didn't have the heart to tell Verna.

"I thaid, 'Why thank you, Perthy old boy.' And he plopped right down and wouldn't budge. Then I thaid, 'C'mon now. THCAT! I have to thweep my back porch.' And do you know what your gran'th old tom did then? Eh heh heh heh."

"There's no tellin'," I conceded as I braced myself for the worst.

"He looked me right in the eye and thaid, 'No!' jutht ath plain ath the nothe on my fathe!"

I slipped my arm around her substantial shoulder and had a good, hearty laugh.

"Don't worry, Verna. He talks to us all the time!"

"Thank goodneth!" Verna exclaimed. And visible relief spread over her features like a salve. "There for a minute…I thought I wath lothing my marblethth!"

"Nah. You still have 'em all," I said reassuringly.

"Tho…who ith taking the little fella home? Eh heh heh heh."

I hesitated a moment before I answered.

"I don't really know if I should. Percy might get the idea…that he's…being replaced. He can be surprisingly sensitive for such a pompous, old windbag."

Verna nodded in agreement. Then she turned to Lily.

"What?" Lily asked dryly.

"Are you taking the little fella home with you? Eh heh heh heh."

"Not likely. I'm not the pet loving type. And besides…I'm not running some flophouse for soggy ragamuffins."

I shot an angry glance at Lily. Sometimes she could be so thoughtless.

"Well…I alwayth have room for one more," Verna said softly. "Did you know that the firtht pet I ever had wath an old Jack Ruththel terrier I rethcued off a roof of a houthe that wath on fire?"

"No, I didn't."

"To thith day I haven't figured out how he got himthelf up on that roof. Yeth, he wath my firtht pet and thtrayth have been theeking me out ever thinthe."

Verna was just a walking bundle of love.

"Oh! Where are my mannerth? How would you two girlth like a little thnack? Eh heh heh heh."

I couldn't help imagining what her idea of a snack might be-two lollipops nestled in a bed of powdered sugar? After all, *something* kept Verna hovering close to four hundred pounds and smiling with a set of teeth that looked like Indian corn.

"Maybe some other time," I answered. "And thanks again for saving the kitten."

"It wath my pleathure," she said.

November

At three in the morning the telephone rang.

"Hullo?"

"This is Sheriff Something-or-other. Lemme talk ta yer dad."

"Da-ad!" I hollered.

"I got it," he answered from somewhere in the dark.

"Bill," the sheriff began, "we found 'er."

I tapped the end of my hairbrush on my nightstand to make it sound as if I'd hung up the phone and then I cupped my right hand tightly over the mouthpiece and continued to listen to their conversation.

"Yeah," the sheriff continued, "one a the busboys found 'er body in a dumpster out behind the truckstop. Damn shame. It coulda been any one a 'er friends. They're a nasty bunch a vermin. One a my men'll get back ta ya." He hesitated about ten seconds before he added, "If I didn't know ya were such a sorry son of a bitch, I could almost feel a twinge a sympathy."

His handset slammed on his receiver.

I had barely hung up when I saw Dad standing in the doorway.

"Were you listenin' on that extension?"

I figured there was no point denying the obvious. "Yeah," I confessed.

"They found your aunt Gladys," he said numbly.

"I heard. Dad…are you gonna tell Gran?"

"Not jus' yet."

"Dad?"

"What, Flowerpot?"

"Why was the sheriff so hateful to you on the phone? I always thought that when there was a death in the family, the sheriff would have to come to your front porch, take off his hat, and be mighty respectful to deliver such bad news."

"I reckon it's just his way. Don't pay it no mind."

I imagined his simple explanation was laden with special meaning, but I knew how useless it would be to press him for any more details. Dad was a man of few words and once he clammed up, he was as locked up and inward-looking as anybody could possibly be. What *had* he done to make the sheriff act like that? I really wanted to know.

On second thought, maybe I didn't. Gran had warned me more than once that it wasn't good to go pryin' into things. She'd said that sometimes it was best just to let sleeping dogs lie.

I didn't *really* need to know.

Yes.

I did.

🍁 🍁 🍁

"Flowerpot?" Gran's frail voice pierced the silence.

"Yeah, Gran, I'm here."

I stepped into the dining room and looked at her silhouette. She lay motionless and moon-eyed in the dimly lit room. Desperately, I hoped that the phone's ringing had been the cause of her being awake. I couldn't bear the thought of her lying around, staring at the ceiling like this at three o'clock *every* morning.

I leaned over and kissed her soft forehead and the smell of warm urine assaulted my nostrils. Then I checked the apparatus that hogged one side of her antique bed. For the past fortnight Gran had been fed through a very small tube in her stomach. Twenty-four hours a day, the machine relentlessly delivered nourishment to her frail body.

Every night after brushing her hair, I had helped her through a simple series of exercises to ease her contractures, but her limbs were still growing more gnarled, despite my best efforts.

"Tell me," she rasped.

"What'd she say?" Dad asked. He had followed me into the dining room and was standing in the doorway, looking at us.

"She wants you to *tell* her."

Dad ran a callused hand through his mop of wavy hair. He walked over to us and clasped Gran's drawn hand.

"Agnes," he said slowly and carefully the way a kindhearted teacher might speak to a very dull child, "Agnes…that was the sheriff on the phone…He found Gladys…She's dead."

I was relieved that he had spared her any lurid details.

"What'd she say?" Dad questioned. "Your gran mumbled somethin' jus' then. It was so soft that I couldn't make it out."

I looked up at him and repeated Gran's last words.

"She said…'I'm free.'"

🍁   🍁   🍁

Tuesday, directly after breakfast we went to the offices of W.G. Dunbarthen, Attorney-at-Law for the reading of Gran's will. My youngest brother, Larry, had driven all the way from Cape just to hear what the old man had to say. Gran hadn't left much to squabble over, and I was glad of it. I'd heard more than my share of horror stories about greedy relatives dividing up the plunder. Dad got her house and most of her stuff and the boys each got an antique quilt. I came out on top; not only did I get an antique quilt, I *also* got to keep Percy.

As we stood up to leave, W.G. cleared his throat.

"Ahem…I'm not entirely finished," he announced. "You may look on this as an odd request…I certainly do, but notwithstanding, it is specified in my client's will and I will perform my duties."

I glanced at Dad. He shrugged.

W.G. continued, "This letter must be read immediately, in the presence of W.G. Dunbarthen. Bill Tait will proceed to answer any questions Senga might have."

He then quickly handed me a plain, white envelope, removed his thick glasses, and polished the lens with his handkerchief.

My name was written on the front of the envelope in small, neat letters. I recognized Gran's handwriting at once. I felt like a creep as I opened that envelope; I knew everyone was staring at me and I never relished that kind of attention.

It was a note from Gran:

My precious Flowerpot,

The people you love will make mistakes and hurt you. They won't mean to, but they will.

You must learn to forgive them and never allow yourself to become bitter.

Yer Champeen,

Gran

The note didn't make any sense. Nobody had *ever* hurt me. I folded it carefully and slid it back into the envelope. I looked up. W.G peered anxiously down at me over the top of his glasses. I glanced at Larry, who seemed angry. Then I looked at Dad.

Dad's mouth stiffened.

"Oh, gah!" he moaned and dropped his head into his hand.

"She has every right to know what kind of a man you are," Larry growled.

Dad slid off his chair and knelt in front of me.

"Senga, I'm sorry…so sorry. I never meant to hurt your mother…or any of you kids. It was a long time ago…back when I use' ta drink my fool head off. And I've made amends. Haven't I made amends? Don't I cook and clean and take good care of you?" he pleaded.

I looked at his careworn face. When had he gotten *so* old? And he was crying! I'd *never* seen him cry before. I was there when he got three fingers torn off during harvest and he hadn't even cried then. Cussed like they say sailors do when they're on shore leave, but not one tear dared to leak out of his eyes. And here he was…kneeling in front of me…and crying like some baby. What in the world did he think was in this note? I hung my head and let my hair fall in front of my face like a flimsy veil.

Dad kept right on talking, but his words seemed muffled and warped, like he was saying them from the bottom of the town pool. He kept at it, but I'd long since stopped listening. I couldn't listen. I hummed away any bogus ideas he tried forcing me to entertain.

I felt his strong hands clamp on both my shoulders, but I still refused to stop humming or look at him.

"Do ya…hate me, Flowerpot?"

"No," I heard myself say. And as soon as I heard myself say it, I knew it must be true.

"Are you gonna be okay?" Larry asked.

"Yeah," I lied.

We had a double funeral that Wednesday. I felt numb, like I was watching myself act out a part in some made-for-television movie. Gran used to have an expression for how I felt. She would've said, "Flowerpot, you look lower than a snake's belly in a wagon rut." That's pretty low. I must've been living on autopilot, 'cause I don't even remember how I made it over to the tree row. A woman I'd never seen before stepped up and latched on to my arm.

"It was a beautiful service," she said.

"Yeah."

"You must be Senga."

"Do I know you?" I heard myself ask.

"No, you don't know me. I've just come to pay my respects."

"Did you know my gran? Or did you come for my aunt Gladys?"

"I knew your gran."

"How'dja know my gran? If ya don't mind me asking."

"Of course I don't mind."

The woman hesitated for a spell before she said, "Your gran was my guardian angel."

I immediately thought of that day at Palmer Slough. I thought of Lily and her belief that someone was always watching over her. I must've looked dumb as a post, 'cause the woman's face softened and she continued.

"I was about your age when I got pregnant."

Gah! Why was a complete stranger telling me something so personal? I wanted to get shed of her and quick.

She continued, "I was so young. The school board had unanimously decided that I couldn't attend classes for the remainder of the school year or graduate with the rest of the class…not in my condition…I was a disgrace. They were afraid pregnancy was contagious…and all of the other girls would wind up with swollen bellies under their gowns."

"Grown-ups can be real peckerwoods," I admitted.

She laughed.

"But…How does my gran fit in with all that?"

"Well…since I wasn't allowed to go to school anymore, your gran took it on herself to tutor me. And the school board gave her hell. Of course, she never told me…She wouldn't have. But then again, she didn't have to. Back then you couldn't even pinch a loaf without everyone knowing what color it was…It got really ugly before it was all said and done. They even viciously attacked your gran's reputation and threatened to fire her…but she never backed down."

"That sounds like my gran. She could be an intrepid old woman when she put her mind to it."

"Because of your grandmother, I got my high school diploma."

"That's great. Good for you!"

"Even after my baby was born, your grandmother continued to watch out for me. She gave me money every month for diapers and food."

The woman stopped talking. She was obviously fighting hard to hold back tears and failing miserably.

"Can you believe that she actually *apologized* to me about the money?"

"Why'd she do that?" I asked.

"She apologized because she couldn't afford to give me *more*. Can you believe that?"

I could and did. Gran would've ripped the shirt clean off her back if she thought someone else could've gotten more use from it.

"Your gran may have thought it was just a little bit a money, but I tell ya what-it meant *everything* to me! I knew your grandfather, Doc, had just passed away and your gran was raising your mother and your aunt Gladys on her paltry teacher's pay. I knew giving me that little dab a money represented a great deal of sacrifice on her part."

The woman dabbed her handkerchief to her red, swollen eyes. Her black mascara was starting to give way, giving her face a raccoon-like appearance.

"After a while, I was able to go out and get a job. I *offered* to repay her, I really did. But she wouldn't hear of it. She just said, 'Don't give it another thought. Everybody needs a little help now and then.'"

By now the woman was crying so hard it sounded like a goose honking. I put my arm around her shoulder.

"I don't know what to say."

She dabbed her handkerchief to her eyes again. Between sniffles, she whispered, "You don't have to say anything. I just wanted you to know…what your grandmother had done for me…and my baby. When I needed someone…she was there. She was my voice…when I couldn't speak up for myself."

In the seventeen years that I'd known Gran, she'd never *once* mentioned this woman, or her baby. If I'd ever done anybody such a good turn, I'd've told anybody and everybody willing to listen.

I had that feeling that someone was staring at me, so I turned around. A young woman I'd never seen before was standing in the tree row, just a foot or two in front of me.

"Hello," she said.

"Hello," I repeated.

The woman clutching my arm smiled proudly and said, "*This* is my baby!"

"Well, I'm awfully glad to meet you," I said. And I meant it. I shook her hand warmly.

"She's in her third year of medical school," the older woman bragged.

"Hush, Momma! You embarrass me."

Then she turned her attention back toward me.

"We brought this for the family," she said softly.

She handed me a beautiful pink kalanchoe in full bloom.

The note simply read, "Thank you."

❦ ❦ ❦

I went home after the service and took my time grooming Percy.

"Down!" he bellowed.

"You're not goin' anywhere. You're gonna sit here like a good cat and let me do you a good turn."

"DOWN!" he repeated.

For Gran's sake, I would *never* allow Percy to have the look of the neglected, his thick coat dirty or unkempt.

December

"YOU HAVE *GOT* TO BE KIDDING," LILY SNAPPED.

"Well, I'm not. With Gran gone…Percy just lays about. It's like his 'get up and go' just got up and went."

"Very funny, Senga. But you know I'm not all that keen on pets littering up the place." She hesitated a full minute as she mulled over my request. "He is housebroken, isn't he?"

"For heaven's sake, Lily, of course he's housebroken!"

I hung up the phone and just shook my head.

Something made me pause on the way out of my house that evening. A still, small voice inside my head whispered, "Don't go!" and for a moment I considered obeying. I carried Percy the entire way to Lily's. A worn out sky bellied over us, plump with the promise of snow. The night was still; the only sound was the wet leaves my footsteps mashed into the sidewalk.

I climbed the two front porch steps and hammered on Lily's door.

"You hungry?" she asked first thing.

"Starving," I confessed.

"There's a bunch of stuff in the pantry. You can just help yourself."

I set Percy on his mat and checked out the pantry. A bunch of stuff she says. Ha! Never in my life had I been presented with such slim pickings! There was a container of microwavable ravioli and a box of bran cereal. The fridge was better. It held a hunk of Colby, six dozen eggs, and half a gallon of milk. I had no problem wolfing down some cereal. No wonder Janelle and Lily were reed thin.

After I'd finished eating, I fished around in my backpack for the treats I'd packed for Percy. I quickly poured out a mound of cheese nibblings for him. He loved cheese nibblings.

❧   ❧   ❧

I washed my hands and carefully measured the dry ingredients Lily had bought that afternoon at the IGA. Then I had to crack and stir the eggs while Lily peeled a small mountain of bananas. Lily had volunteered to bake six dozen muffins for the Holiday Angel Bake Sale. (She was desperate for the ten points of extra credit in our civics class.)

"Why the long face?" Lily asked.

"I don't have a long face."

"Of course you do," she argued.

"I really don't want to talk about it."

"Well?" Lily demanded.

Something about her expression led me to believe that she wasn't used to hearing the word NO.

I sat quietly and stirred the eggs.

"You *are* going to tell me what's bothering you."

"I'm lost without Gran," I finally admitted.

"Oh."

"I didn't think it was possible…to miss someone so much."

"What do you miss about her?"

"*Everything*. She's always *been* there. Not a single day of my life has passed…without her planted somewhere in the background, cheering me on. She was my champeen. And the worst part is that she won't even be there to watch me graduate. I wanted her to be in the audience when Superintendent Palmer handed me my diploma. I wanted to give her my rose."

"Your rose?"

"You'll see. Every year the graduates get to go out to the audience and give their rose to those responsible for seeing 'em through to the end."

"That is so sweet. I've been to several graduations and I've never seen anything like that."

"Well...it is a small school. I reckon ya couldn't do that sort a thing at a big school. It would be a chore just to read off all the names...at a big school."

"More than anything...I wanted Gran to be in that audience."

"Maybe not in *person*. But...maybe God...lets the good grandmothers watch special events on Earth...you know...from up in Heaven. It could happen," Lily said.

I couldn't believe my ears. I knew what Lily *really* thought about God, and the church, and everything that smacked of religion. I knew Lily was trying to be comforting, even though she wasn't all that good at it.

"Too bad you never got to meet Gran before she went downhill. She was so funny, Lily. I think you really would've liked her. And once she got goin'...she could talk the hind leg off a mule. All of my life...she talked and I took notes. But...close to the end, I was the one who had to do all of the talking. She didn't say much of anything...and even the little bit she did manage to say seemed to take...such effort."

I turned my face away from Lily and Percy so that I could wipe away the tears that had puddled up.

"What now?" Lily asked.

"Nothin'. I musta...got some flour in my eye," I lied.

"I'm sure you did," Lily said. Her tone was too soft to be sarcastic.

I managed to pull myself together and put on a brave face. I turned my face back toward Lily and Percy and PLAP! A well-aimed spoonful of mashed banana had hit its mark.

"Hey! Whadja have ta go and do that for?"

But Lily didn't answer. Instead, she quietly and relentlessly pelted me with spoonfuls of sticky, mashed banana.

I was too surprised to defend myself. Sloppy blobs of mashed banana dropped off my face and hair and shoulders onto the linoleum floor. I had to scrape the thick, slimy mess from my eyes and nose between guffaws.

"You don't have a long face anymore," Lily proudly announced.

And I was laughing too hard to stay mad at her.

🍁   🍁   🍁

"What're we gonna do now?"

"*We* are going to bake six dozen banana nut muffins, just like I promised. I *have* to get that extra credit."

"But...but, you've just ruined all of the bananas! Did you buy any extra?"

"No."

"Well, I know *I* don't have any at my house and the IGA doesn't open till nine tomorrow morning. We have to have the muffins dropped off by *eight!*"

The situation seemed desperate. I trained my eyes on Lily.

"Ring a ding ding," she said.

I surveyed the damage. Slick banana was still oozing down the wall to my left, leaving a dull trail. And slimy dollops were hanging tenaciously to the blue goose curtains to my right.

"What a mess! What're ya gonna tell Janelle?"

"The truth of course. Just give me a couple of minutes to come up with it."

But as luck would have it, Janelle appeared at the kitchen doorway.

"What was that weird noise?" She asked.

Janelle seemed frozen in time, framed in the doorway with her arms akimbo.

"What...in...the world..."

Instinctively, Lily stood up.

"Lily! There's something *slimy* dripping off my new goose curtains!" Janelle roared.

Lily put on a morbid expression and walked over to Janelle. She spoke so softly I could scarcely hear.

"Senga's grandmother just died. It was so traumatic, they didn't even celebrate Thanksgiving this year."

Lily shot me a look of sympathy.

"I guess she's just not handling it very well."

Janelle glanced my way; convinced that I was the culprit.

Damn Lily's hide! With a few words, she had managed to turn the whole thing around and pin this entire fiasco on me!

"I'll clean up *everything*, Janelle. You don't have to worry."

"I trust you, Lily Billy." Janelle glanced at me again.

I felt red hot and guilty for something I hadn't even done.

"I'll be out late, so don't wait up."

🍁   🍁   🍁

As Janelle's car tires crunched the gravel in the driveway, I watched Lily scrape mashed bananas off the linoleum floor, her hand a makeshift spatula. She plopped the salvaged mess into the mixing bowl.

"We're short."

She set the bowl in front of me and leaned over and squeezed mashed banana from my hair until it drizzled down to join the rest.

"We're still short. We're going to have to add extra applesauce to make up the difference."

"What're you talkin' about?"

"You heard me."

"We can't do this," I pleaded.

"Sure we can. And we will."

She was unfazed.

"These are decent folk, Lily."

"*Decent folk,*" she mimicked. "Pa-*leeze*. Decent folks don't go around battering a pillowcase full of kittens."

She had a point. And for a split second, I actually considered going along for the ride, but then the voice of reason was back at the helm.

"Look, Lily, I just can't do this. Friends of Dad's and Gran's will be there. They don't deserve to have hair or grit or whatall nastyin' up their baked goods."

I half expected Lily to turn on me and call me a coward or a weakling or much worse. Instead she just rolled her soft brown eyes at me-her dismissal of choice.

"Big deal. I'll do it all by myself, so you can keep that precious conscience of yours crystal clear, but don't you dare sit there and tell me that these *decent folks* don't need a bit of hair in their muffins."

To emphasize her passion, she jabbed me with her perfectly manicured index finger as she added, "They're just lucky I don't stir in a handful of mouse droppings and call them raisins."

I was convinced that Lily had completely lost her mind.

❦   ❦   ❦

In no time, the kitchen was back to normal. Lily had kept her word to Janelle. She had scoured the room thoroughly and hadn't let me lift a finger to help. She even threw Janelle's new goose curtains into the washing machine.

❦   ❦   ❦

"I know the perfect solution for a stressed out girl," Lily said. "Something sweet…definitely chocolate! I snagged two chocolate bars at the IGA this afternoon."

"I didn't think you ever indulged. There's not an ounce of fat anywhere on your body."

"Just a bite now and then never hurt anybody. Besides, didn't you know that when you spell STRESSED backwards, you come up with DESSERTS?"

Gran musta known that. She used to just *love* chocolates...especially Russell Stover's. What was it she always used to say? Oh, yeah. "When your sweet tooth says *chocolate*, your wisdom tooth whispers *Russell Stover.*"

🍁 🍁 🍁

The muffins were baked and set out to cool. I decided it would be easier to wash the stickiness out of my hair standing in the shower than lurching over the kitchen sink.

I always let Percy stay in the bathroom with me whenever I was in there. (He is the only cat I ever met who actually seemed to enjoy water.) In the shower, I was surprised to see a fine crescent cut on my chest. Lily's fingernail had drawn blood. Nearly finished rinsing the conditioner out of my hair, I felt a sudden draft. Lily had pulled back the curtain and was standing directly behind me in the shower.

"How about it?" she inquired.

I didn't answer.

"Are you afraid...that I'm one of those girls *normal* people whisper about under their breath?"

I quickly got out of the shower and wrapped myself in a Turkish towel.

"Why? Are you?"

"No. I was just messing with you. Sheesh, Senga! Have you already forgotten how ridiculously small the hot water tank is in this old house? I can't tell you how many times Janelle and I have almost come to blows over it. I just wanted you to shove out and leave me some hot water."

I felt like a complete fool. I bent over and wound a smaller towel around my wet hair. And that's when I *saw it*.

A prosthetic foot was carefully propped up against the bathtub.

"Lily, did you..."

"Yes, I heard it too."

She was answering a question I hadn't even asked. She cut off the water, flung back the shower curtain, and stepped out of the shower. I was mindful not to stare. Her right leg stopped neatly above the ankle. She squatted and fastened the prosthesis in place. Then she quickly stood up and motioned for her robe.

I couldn't help wondering what had happened to my friend.

"Lily, did you remember to lock the doors before we came up here?"

Her eyes grew wide at my question.

"Of course I did. Oh! Senga, I *think* I did. I know I locked the front door. I just...I just can't remember if I locked the back door."

Suddenly Percy stiffened. He turned his blind eyes to the bathroom door as a guttural growl emanated from somewhere deep inside. The primal sound caused goosebumps to rise on our wet bodies.

"Someone's downstairs," I said. "And I don't think it's Janelle."

"We've got to get to my bedroom. The lock on that door actually works."

We quickly crept to Lily's bedroom and locked her door. Together we shoved her heavy hope chest in front of it.

"Hey! Percy's still out there!" I gasped and struggled to heave the chest away from the door.

"Are you nuts? There is *no* way I'm going to let you open that door! Not even for your gran's old cat."

"He's *my* cat now."

"I don't care whose cat he is. You are not opening that door!"

My stomach sank. I would've rescued Percy, but Lily pinned me to the wall the way a wrestler pins his opponent to the mat. I was amazed at her strength.

"Where'd ya learn a move like that?" I asked, panting and red faced.

"Never mind."
Clumsy footsteps clambered up the old stair treads.
"I *have* to see what's goin' on!" I begged.
"Promise you won't open that door, no matter *what* you see."
I hesitated.
"PROMISE!" Lily demanded.
"All right. I promise. Now lemme go."

I pressed my eye against the old keyhole. I could see the landing. And I could see Percy. He stood fixed, unmovable. Eighteen pounds of feline fury guarded that bedroom door that night. He was protecting me, protecting us from an enemy he couldn't even see.

"Li-ly…Li-ly…Li-ly," the stranger's thin voice swelled in crescendo as he grew closer and closer to her locked bedroom door.

I turned to her.

"Do you *know* him?"

"I don't think so. I don't recognize that voice."

"Li-ly, I had to ssssssee you."

It was the slurred speech of a drunk.

"OUT!" Percy wailed.

It sounded like the fierce warning was torn from his throat.

"Li-ly…"

"NOW!" Percy roared.

"What the…lemme go…you damn cat!" the stranger yelled.

His outrage at being bitten was followed by the dull FLUMP of Percy's solid body slamming against the wall.

My heart rose up in my throat and lodged there.

"You are *not* opening that door!" Lily reminded me through clenched teeth.

My eye remained plastered to that keyhole.

"Li-ly…c'mere. I jus'…wanna…talk to ya," the intruder slurred.

"Are you *sure* you don't know who that is out there? He sure seems to know you. How in the devil does he know your name?"

Lily didn't answer.

"Well, get down here, quick! Look through this keyhole and see if his face might jog your memory."

Lily quickly obeyed.

"He sure is a mushroomy clodhopper," I whispered in Lily's ear.

"Oh, sheesh! It's that neighbor of Cathy's."

"So you *do* know him."

"Yes. I mean…no. Well, I don't really *know* him. He lives next door to Cathy…in Poplar Bluff. I met him last summer…when Janelle and I stopped by to visit her new baby."

"Why'dya think he's out there?"

"I have no idea. I don't even know how he found out where I live. I certainly wouldn't have told him.…not in a million years."

"Listen! Didja hear that?" I asked (and was surprised at the froggy croak of my own voice).

Lily stared at me in anticipation. We were in a state to be scared at every sound.

She shook her head NO in two quick jerks.

"I didn't hear anything."

"Sh! There it is again."

We both heard it that time. It sounded like quick, light footfalls moving through the house and now coming up the stairs.

"That *must* be Janelle!" Lily exclaimed. "She's always been so light on her feet; I could recognize her airy footsteps anywhere. She'll sort this whole mess out."

Relieved, we deftly moved the chest away from the bedroom door and Lily swung it open, ready to spring to Janelle's aid.

"Thank God!" Lily exclaimed.

🍁   🍁   🍁

But it *wasn't* Janelle.

❧   ❧   ❧

Two strange men were now standing on the upper landing!

❧   ❧   ❧

I froze.

Lit from behind, Lily's face was in the shadow, so I couldn't make out her expression, but her fear was palpable. Urine streamed down her legs and she stood, as if in a trance, in the warm puddle.

The older man was unusually tall. He was wearing a BDU jacket, and I had the foggy notion that I'd seen him somewhere before. With one swift motion, he subdued the other, younger man and managed to sling him over his shoulder like a sack of produce. He brushed past Lily and me and went directly to Lily's bedroom window. And with his free hand, he pulled down her window blinds. Then he turned around and left—without saying a word. He descended the stairs gracefully two at a time, despite his awkward burden.

I cut off the light and stepped over to the window. Carefully, I lifted a blind, peeked out, and saw the lumpy figure disappear into the tangle of trees, becoming one more shadow in the night. Snow began to fall-a mantle of white to cover the night's nefarious deeds.

I left the window and looked at my friend.

"Step back," I said gently.

Like a child, Lily obeyed.

I unwound the towel from my damp hair and used it to sop up the urine. She crumpled on the floor beside her bed and bore the look of a scared rabbit being conjured up out of a magician's black hat.

"You won't *tell* anybody…about me…peeing on myself, will you?"

"Nah. It ain't nobody's business. Besides, everybody needs a little help now and then."

She forced a weak smile.

I let out a dry laugh.

"So you think it's funny?" She asked. She sounded hurt.

"No, Lily. I don't think it's funny. It's just a bad habit I have. I always laugh when I'm nervous."

I took the soiled towel to the bathroom and dropped it into the bathtub. When I came back into the bedroom, Lily was sitting up, more composed, more like her usual self.

"Lily?"

"What?"

"That old guy saved us."

"I know."

※　　　※　　　※

"C'mon, Lily. We're gonna hafta go downstairs and make sure all of the doors are locked."

"And the windows," she added.

"And the windows," I repeated.

※　　　※　　　※

We didn't sleep a wink that night.

We did what we could for Percy, but even he had only nine lives.

※　　　※　　　※

At eight the next morning, we promptly delivered six dozen banana nut muffins to Mrs. Chantle, the bake sale chairwoman. My heart was thumping so loudly, I was certain everyone in Butler County could hear it. To the ignorant, I'm sure those muffins appeared pretty, sitting on that table, bundled up in their pastel plastic wrap; but to me, the hair and grit stood out like vile obscenities.

As we were leaving, Lily clutched my arm and whispered into my ear, "Look! There he is!"

I turned to look by the double doors. She was right. The man in the BDU jacket had come to the bake sale!

Lily and I exchanged knowing glances.

"He barged right into your room last night and pulled down your window blinds. Why'dya s'pose he'd do a thing like that?" I asked.

"How should I know?"

Then she gave me a sweet conspiring smile.

"Let's get out of here."

January

Looking back, it had been a tough year. I hadn't expected much of anything from Christmas, so I wasn't all that disappointed. It had been a lot harder on Dad. Pork prices had bottomed out and it seemed he was getting less for a whole hog than it cost to buy a canned ham at the IGA. And yet, he had fared better than most. I had to hand it to him. He had done his homework and besides the hogs, he had experimented with niche crops. He had repeated the word "Diversification" as if it were a mantra. (That was the most syllables I'd ever heard him use, and it made my heart proud.) We never had to sin to eat; and although he always managed to put food on the table, we both knew his farming days were numbered.

❋   ❋   ❋

The holidays were over, and the air had hardened toward frost. This time of the year always settled me into a pensive mode. I liked to think. And I did my best thinking as I walked alongside Palmer Slough.

❋   ❋   ❋

"Didja like your Christmas present?" I asked.

"I thought they smelled wonderful. Good enough to eat. I set them on the bathroom counter so Janelle could share the wealth," Lily answered.

(I had wrapped up the fancy fruit soaps I'd gotten two Christmases before. The tag was still on; so technically the gift was brand new. Lily was none the wiser.)

"Did you?"

"Yeah. She's real cute. I'd never even heard of a corn dolly till you gave me one."

"It was handmade especially for you, Senga. Janelle had one of her English friends send it over from Essex."

Lily waved her fingers rhythmically in the air, in front of my face like she was casting a spell.

"But you don't have to worry; I'm certain they didn't imbue that corn dolly with any mystical powers."

"Took a load off my mind."

"You won't believe what Janelle gave *me* for Christmas!"

I pretended to be interested although I secretly hated the one-up-man-ship brought on by Christmas mornings. It seemed like we *never* had any extra money kicking about, so I'd learned to be content with hand-knitted mittens, scarves, and hats, or underwear-infinitely practical gifts. I'd endured a litany over the years by various friends about their holiday haul of designer clothes and trinkets that had been bestowed on them by grandparents and aunts and uncles, so I reckoned "Thou shalt not covet" was the hardest commandment of them all to keep intact.

"Well, aren't you even going to guess?" Lily urged.

Here I go again.

"Hmmm, a zebra?"

"Be serious, Senga. What in the world would I do with a zebra? Think practical, will you?"

"A hand-knitted hat and scarf," I shot back.

Lily moaned.

"I said *practical*, not *bore me to tears*. Okay. I'll give you a little clue. Think *college*."

Then it hit me. Janelle had given Lily the dream of every American teenager-a car.

"A car?" I felt a lump of pure jealousy rise in my throat.

"A car? I wish! No, Senga. Janelle gave me my very first credit card. Isn't that excellent? Now I'm all set for college."

Big deal, I thought. Percy got pre-approved credit cards all of the time.

"Well…I'd a never guessed," was all I could say.

🍁   🍁   🍁

"Now that's weird."

"What is?"

"The lightning hole. It's all filled up. You and Janelle didn't do it, didja?"

"Of course not," Lily said. "The lightning hole…What are you talking about?"

"The *lightning* hole…Oh! I'm sorry…I guess you wouldn't know anything about it."

She shrugged and then raised her left eyebrow in anticipation.

"See here?"

I pointed at two slippery elms and the obvious gaping space between them.

"Last spring lightning struck the one in the middle and burned it down to the ground. Burned it right down to the *roots*! There was a good size hole here for the longest. Then the Miller's dogs kept diggin' at it and made it a lot bigger. You sure Janelle didn't come out here and fill it in?" I asked again. I wanted to be sure.

"She would've told me. Besides, she's not really the gardening type."

"D'ya s'pose…?"

"What?"

"I was jus' thinkin'…that maybe…"

"You think that old codger in the BDU jacket *killed* that boy and dumped his body in this hole?"

"I dunno. I hope not. But he…did…look kinda dead, the way he was slung over that man's shoulder. I didn't hear one sound outta him as he was being lugged down your stairs that night! And I *did* see them come this way. Remember? I watched them from your bedroom window."

"Sheesh! You have one overactive imagination."

"Ya think so? Ya think I'm just bein' creepy? Then why is this hole all filled in like this?"

"How should I know! Maybe somebody from the town…a maintenance man or something, came and filled it in."

"Not likely. This is private property. It's an uphill climb to get Terrence out to scrape a dead cat off the road when it needs doin'. There's no way he'd *volunteer* ta come out here and fill in this hole or do any other type of work."

"Sheesh!"

"What's wrong? Are you having a Charlie horse or something?"

"No, I'm not having a Charlie horse."

"A cramp?"

"No, it's not a cramp. It's my foot! It's itching like mad!"

Lily squatted and unfastened her prosthesis.

"Remind me to get this fixed," she said.

"Get what fixed?" I asked.

"This fastener. It's never been this loose before and I'm afraid if I don't get it fixed soon, it's going to pop off."

I eyed the contraption and stroked my chin the way I'd seen Gran do over the years.

"Where'dja go ta get somethin' like that fixed?"

"Janelle knows a man in Poplar Bluff."

"Tell me somethin', Lily," I stalled, fumbling for the right set of words. "How could a foot…that doesn't even exist…possibly *itch*?"

"I know it sounds crazy."

I didn't say anything. I just stood there wondering how she could possibly make sense out of something so senseless.

"It is crazy, isn't it? I can't really explain. It just itches. And sometimes it itches like mad! *Like right now.* Janelle calls it my 'little phantom foot.' I swear, Senga, it'll be the end of me one day."

"What happened to you?" I asked.

"You mean the foot thing?"

I nodded.

"No big deal," she answered nonchalantly. "I was born like this."

At that moment, I wanted to ask her a million different questions. What was it like? Did it hurt? Did she run and jump and have both of her feet at night, in her dreams? But I didn't ask a single one. I didn't want Lily to be uncomfortable and I didn't want her to feel that I was making it into a federal case.

She stood up and winked at me.

"Tell you what…Sen-ga, if this hole bothers you that much…let's come out here tonight…and dig out all of that dirt. That way, we can see what's what. We can settle your suspicions once and for all."

"You'd do that for me?"

"Of course," she said, without a moment's hesitation.

I was genuinely touched.

🍁 🍁 🍁

At midnight, we met behind Lily's garage.

"D'ya think we can do this all in one stitch?" I asked. "Are ya absolutely positive ya still wanna go through with it?" I wanted to give her the chance to dodge out gracefully. And I didn't want to find any dead body at the bottom of that hole.

"Of course I want to go through with it. Why else would I have snagged Janelle's flashlight? I see that you remembered to bring the shovel."

I nodded.

"What are you doing with that thing?" Lily asked.

"It's my old baton. I thought I'd probe the ground before we commence diggin.'"

"Well, well, well...I would've never figured you for the majorette type."

"I wasn't. Practically all us girls took baton lessons at the armory when we were in grade school. Maybe all that time wasn't wasted after all."

We walked in silence to the slough. Our footprints glistened in the fine layer of snow.

"Do you feel anything? Inquiring minds...you know."

I stopped probing and looked squarely at Lily. She could be so goofy when she thought no one was watching.

"Nah, not yet."

"And here we are without our team of cadaver sniffing dogs!"

"Knock it off, Lily. You're creepin' me out."

I continued to probe...systematically. I didn't want to miss anything.

"Looks like...we hit the jackpot."

"What? Is it...mushy? Or does it feel like an arm or a leg? Sheesh, Senga! Don't poke that silly baton of yours into an eye socket..."

I froze.

"Oh! Stop gnashing your teeth, you scaredy cat. I was just messing with you."

"Sh! I thought I heard someone cough."

"Well, I didn't hear anything."

"Sh! Listen! There it was again."

I cocked my head to one side and trained my eyes south, toward Winding Way, where a figure moved in the dark.

The *sensible* thing to do was run, but Lily and I seemed rooted to the spot. And *He* was beside us before I could even pull my old baton up out of the ground.

Lily had the presence of mind to slyly tilt the flashlight up so we could steal a glance at who it was we were dealing with. It was the tall man in the BDU jacket. He fixed his soft brown eyes on Lily.

"Go home," he said. "You girls have no business around here."

February

I reckon I should've been thrilled about the Valentine's Dance the way the other girls were, but I simply couldn't get myself to register anything. Too much had happened in too short a time and I felt like a zombie inside.

I was dog-tired and just about to climb into my bed when I first heard the rhythmic tapping on the window glass. TAP. TAP. TAP. There was a space of silence for about fifteen seconds before I heard it again. TAP. TAP. TAP. I cut off the light and crept over to my window. Surreptitiously, I pulled the curtain back and peered outside. Quietly, I slid up the sash.

"*Jasmine*! What the devil are you doin' creepin' around out there?"

"Let me in, Senga."

"Now why would I wanna do that?"

"C'mon, Senga. Let me in."

She nervously looked over her shoulder into the dark Missouri night as if she were afraid she had been followed.

"Oh! All right, but make it snappy."

After she crawled through my window, I pulled it shut and waited for some solid explanation.

She forced a smile and said, "*Nobody* calls me Jasmine anymore."

"Sorry, Jazz. I guess I forget sometimes."

"It's okay, Senga. I bet you're wonderin' why *I'm* here."

"Yeah."

"I wanted to tell ya somethin'. Well, first I wanted to ask ya somethin', and then I wanted to tell ya somethin'."

"Well, Jazz, it looks like you have my undivided attention, so start talkin'. I'm all ears."

"Are you goin' to the Valentine's Dance?"

"Maybe. Why would you care?"

"You'd better not go," Jazz warned.

"And why's that?"

"If you go, Red means to hurt you," she said.

"Red don't scare me," I lied. "I can take care a myself."

Jazz leaned close and I caught a glimpse of the old Jasmine in her steady eyes.

"Now you listen to me, Senga Tait, and you listen good. If you go to that dance, *Red means to hurt you.*"

"Jus' what're you sayin'?"

I looked deep into her eyes and without her saying another word, I knew *exactly* what it was she was trying to tell me.

"And just why're you tellin' me? I thought you and Red were tight."

"Man, Senga, to be so smart you sure are dumb. There's a great big world a stuff you don't know."

"Yeah?"

"Yeah."

"Well...since you came all the way over here in the dead of night, maybe you'd like to educate me."

She let out a sardonic laugh.

"Me educate you...what a trick that would be. What is it you're so keen on knowin'?"

"We...used to be friends...right?"

"You *know* we did."

"Well...what did I ever do...to make you hate me so much?"

"I don't hate you, Senga. You might not believe that, but it's the God's honest truth! I never did hate you...and I don't think...I ever could. There's just a whole lot of stuff you don't understand. Or maybe you don't even know."

"Then why'dya hang around with that beast?"

"It's complicated," Jazz said.

"Nothin' could be all that complicated."

Jazz looked down at her faded jeans and sighed.

"I'm not goin' anywhere," she explained.

"What?"

"Oh, hell, Senga! Everybody knows you're gettin' outta here. We've all known it since the fourth grade. You and Harrison will ditch this ol' town just as soon as you graduate. And you know it as well as I do.... *But I'll still be here!* I'm not goin' anywhere. And Red's not goin' anywhere either. Don't you get it?"

❦   ❦   ❦

I was beginning to.

❦   ❦   ❦

"Well then…can you tell me this…why does *Red* hate me so much?"

"You really don't have a clue, do you?"

Instinctively, I shrugged.

"It's on account a yer dad."

"Dad? What's he got to do with Red hating my guts?"

"It's nothin' at all ta do with you. It started way before you were even born. Your dad…had an affair with Red's mom."

Jazz gave me a minute to let her words sink in.

"Why did you *think* your mother killed herself?"

I reeled as if an icy hand had slapped my face.

"MY MOTHER DID NOT KILL HERSELF!"

"Oh, God, Senga! You can't be that stupid. *Nobody* can live as long as you have and be that stupid."

"I'm not stupid."

I felt my hands ball into two, ready fists.

"Are you standin' there tellin' me you *really didn't* know?"

"I'm not tellin' you anything…except…You're just plain full of crap."

"You really didn't know…Hey, I'm sorry, Senga."

"Dad told me that my mother died 'cause there was somethin' wrong with her heart."

"There was. That two-timing louse broke it when he cheated on her with Red's mom."

"Don't call him that!"

"Sometimes the truth hurts," Jazz said with an indifferent shrug.

"Dad also told me that my mother died quickly…that she didn't…suffer much."

"If you consider drowning yourself not suffering much, well then, I guess he was telling you the truth."

"How'd you come to know so much about *my* mother?"

"Red told me."

"Red's nothin' but a big, fat liar."

"Oh! It's the truth all right. Red overheard her dad talkin' to one of his deputies about it, but he has no idea that she even knows. The whole town knows how much the sheriff despises your dad, but only a handful knows *why*. Senga, the sheriff must have a gen-u-ine soft spot for you or else he wouldn't have kept the whole mess a secret for all of these years."

I could not believe what I was hearing.

"How does *he* know?" I demanded.

"Well, he *is* the sheriff," Jazz replied. "And he *was* the one…who found her body."

"I have to sit down," I said.

"Yeah, I guess you'd better. Red told me all about it as soon as she found out. Your mom killed herself a few days after you were born. If you don't believe her, or me, you can always look it up at the library. They keep all of the old newspapers and stuff like that."

"I thought you said the sheriff kept it all a secret? If it was in the newspaper, it surely wasn't a big secret. And...what? Is *everybody* in on it? Are you tellin' me that I'm the only person in this entire town who doesn't know what happened? Gah! And it was *my* mother!"

"What I meant was...your mom's death *was* in the paper, but it was listed as a heart attack. The story of how the sheriff came to find your mom's body *is* in the newspaper though. I know it's true, Senga. Red and I went to the library and read it for ourselves."

The headlines blared:

HACKETT HITS THE HANDRAIL

"Well...what did it say?"

"I'm not gonna sit here an' recite the whole thing for ya, word for word. But if ya really want ta read it for yourself, I'll show ya exactly where ta find it."

"Well...can you at least give me the gist of it?"

"It had rained...all that night before, making the roads slicker 'an cat shit. Old man Hackett lost control of his battery-powered wheelchair on the bridge. An' there was a photograph of him sitting on his red scooter, kinda like a BEFORE photo, I guess. He didn't have any hair then either...just in case you were wonderin'. He skidded so bad that he lost control...drove his pride and joy smack into Palmer Slough! Then he pitched such a hissy fit that the sheriff was forced to drag the slough until he found the dumb ol' thing."

I listened quietly as Jazz recounted the newspaper article.

"The sheriff found it all right, but not until he found your mother's body first."

"She must've been in a bad way to go and do somethin' like that. Sheriff said she had four cinder blocks tied to her ankles...And once those blocks sank in the muddy bottom of the slough, she didn't stand a chance."

My body felt like lead.

"But he kept it a secret, all a these years. The newspaper just mentioned that your mom was found in the slough. Apparently she had had a heart attack and had somehow managed to fall in. He didn't breathe a word about the cinder blocks tied around her ankles. That part *wasn't* in the paper. That's the part Red heard him talking about on the telephone. Are you listenin' ta me, Senga?"

I started to hum. If I hummed it couldn't be true. *It couldn't be true!* I would sit on my bed and hum forever…so it could *never* be true.

"Now you know why I had to come over. Red *hates* you. She blames you for *everything*."

"Are you even listening ta me?"

I continued to hum.

"Red's mom stuck around for a while, but then hooked up with some insurance salesman from St. Louis. *I* know it wasn't your doin' and *you* know that, but Red isn't always logical…Are you gettin' any of this, Senga?"

I didn't answer.

I couldn't answer.

"Red's suffered too, ya know…"

"How could you even say that to me?"

"'Cause it's the God's honest truth, that's why. Haven't ya ever noticed the thick make-up she wears?"

"So what. I jus' reckoned she was no slave to fashion."

"She's not covering up any zits…she's got a flawless complexion," Jazz hinted.

"What're you talkin' about?"

"You can't possibly be that stupid, Senga. The sheriff beats her. She wears the make-up jus' to cover up the bruises."

"Who told you that?"

"Look…I don't have all a that *book knowledge* cloudin' up my brain. I got eyes. I can see for myself."

"Well, if that's the truth, why doesn't Red jus' tell on him and be done with it?" I asked.

"*Who's she gonna tell?*"

(That was the first time in my life I'd ever felt sorry for Red.)

"And that ain't even the worst part. The sheriff sticks it to her every chance he gets."

"What?"

"Listen, Senga, I gotta go. Are you gonna be okay?"

I rocked back and forth and refused to answer her.

"Stop humming and listen to me! You gotta swear…SWEAR you'll never breathe a word of this to another living soul…'cause if you do…and Red catches wind of it…I can't *imagine*…what she might do ta me."

Jazz must've let herself out of my bedroom window.

I forced myself to keep her awful news in some sort of perspective. And I took her advice. There was no way I would spoil Harrison's evening on account of Red, especially after he had already shelled out a wad to rent his tuxedo for the night. I reckoned if I couldn't *go* to the Valentine's Dance, then I would *bring* it to me. And sweet, trusting Harrison didn't ask any questions.

"C'mon in and let me hang up your coat. WOW! You look beautimus!"

"Beautimus?" Lily repeated. "Is that a euphemism?"

"Nah, it just means you look *way* past beautiful."

She spun around slowly so that I could admire her.

"Do you think I could score one direct hit on your cousin's sensory apparatus?"

"Lily! Why wouldja wanna go and say somethin' like that?"

She smiled seductively and didn't answer.

"Thanks for coming over tonight."

"Fine with me. You knew nobody asked me to the school dance." She fiddled with the revealing neckline of her bodice. "You didn't decide to stay home 'cause of me, did you?"

"Nah. I never liked ya that much!"

We laughed.

"I brought you something," Lily said as she reached into her canvas tote.

"My baton!"

"Yes, ma'am."

"You went *back*?"

"Of course I went back. It takes more than some bossy old codger who shops in a military surplus store to scare me away."

(Gran would've adored Lily.)

"And you aren't going to believe what I dug up."

She paused for effect.

"Well?

She just stood there with her left eyebrow arched mysteriously.

"Wouldn't you like to know?"

"Do I have to drag it out of you?" I pleaded.

"You were right all along."

"Gah!"

"I probed around with your baton…until I hit something soft and mushy."

Suspense seized my imagination.

"What did you do then?" I asked.

"Well, since I was fresh out of cadaver-sniffing dogs, I did the next best thing. I started digging."

"I would've been scared to death!" I confessed.

"*Nothing* could've scared me more than seeing those two men on my landing that night. Besides, what could some dead guy possibly do to me? I don't believe in spooks."

"Did you tell the sheriff yet? You know…We're gonna have ta tell the sheriff."

"No, I didn't tell the sheriff."

"Lily…Why not?"

"I would just come off looking like a complete fool."

I didn't understand.

"But…why?"

At this, Lily threw her head back and let out a delectable laugh.

"What?" I demanded.

"I dug up…six dozen…banana nut muffins…in pastel plastic wrap."

"Nah!"

"It's true," Lily said firmly.

"*You're crazy!*"

"I swear, Senga. If I'm lyin', I'm dyin'."

"Then…that man's crazy, isn't he?"

"Maybe he is, maybe he isn't. I haven't decided. People do weird stuff every day of the week. Who am I to judge?"

"But whyddya think he'd do somethin' like that?"

"We saw him at the bake sale. Maybe he bought the muffins, took a big bite and got a mouthful of grit."

"I don't buy it. I could see him buying one muffin or maybe two. If he bit into something unsavory, he probably would've just thrown the muffin into the trashcan or down the garbage disposal. I mean, that's what any *normal* person would do. I know that's what I would do."

"Yeah, that makes sense."

"Why would he buy *all six dozen* muffins? That's too weird. It's almost like…"

"What?"

"It's almost like he had been...*watching* what we did. It's like he knew that we did something stupid that could've gotten us into trouble."

"That's too creepy! But..."

"But what?" Lily demanded.

"But...it kinda makes sense. Or how could he have possibly known that there was an intruder in your house? Unless...he had been watching...Who knows what that young clodhopper would've tried on you if that man hadn't been...watching you all evening."

"This is one weird little burg. I thought you said that nothing ever happens around here."

"Nothing ever did. Not until you an' Janelle drove into town."

"Enough about that," Lily announced, deliberately changing the subject. "You told me to bring my favorite food, so I made a fancy cheese and cracker platter with little pickles and olives. I even sneaked out a jar of Janelle's beluga caviar!"

"Thanks, Lily. I hope the boys remember to bring something...edible."

"Now turn around," Lily admonished. "SLOWLY. I want to see your new dress. Well...well...well. I had no idea you were so...*domestic*."

"Ah, Gran taught me how to sew when I was still in grade school."

"You look *great!*"

"Thanks. What is it? By the expression on your face, you almost look...you do! You look...*Relieved*! Gah! Whadja think I was gonna wear? My overalls? Gee, Lily, ya gotta give me some credit."

"Sorry. But I've never seen you...dressed like..."

"-a female?"

"Hey, I said I was sorry."

"It's okay, Lily. I don't wear a dress unless I have to."

"Maybe you should."

"Nah. Can you get the door while I set out the food? It's prob'ly just Harrison, but look through the peephole first. I don't want any surprises tonight."

"Will do."

"Good evening, Harrison," Lily said formally.

"Hey, Lily. You look nice tonight."

"Thank you."

"Hey, Senga," Harrison whispered as he planted a soft kiss on my cheek. "I brought ya a little something. It's a corsage. An' I hope ya like it."

"Of course I like it. I'd like anything you gave me."

He carefully pinned it to the left side of my dress.

"Thanks, Harry. Oh! You are *so* sweet ta me. Pretty *and* they smell good too. Lily, smell this."

"Umm. Nice," she said.

"*And* I brought a bunch of pizza rolls in this plastic tub," Harrison said.

"Cousin Duane called earlier. He might be a bit late."

🍁 　　　🍁 　　　🍁

"Lily, I'd like ya ta meet Cousin Duane."

She offered him her hand the way the royal ladies do in those grainy black and white movies. He promptly accepted, lifted it delicately to his mouth, and brushed the back of it with his lips. He was wearing one of those tee shirts that had been airbrushed to look like a tuxedo. (He was an eyeful, even though he was my cousin). He gingerly released Lily's hand and then ran his right hand through his dark, wavy hair.

"Flowerpot, I brought some root beer," he finally said.

"Thanks. Here. Lemme get that."

"I think I figured out why y'all are holed up like this. It's Brillo Queen. Isn't it? Jus' say the word, Flowerpot and I'll whoop her ass!"

(Nothing got passed Cousin Duane.)

"Better not," Lily casually remarked. "If you whoop Red's ass, she might enjoy it too much."

"I like her already," Cousin Duane said as he glanced at Lily.

I would've sworn she blushed.

🍁   🍁   🍁

"Lily, you mean to tell me you've *never* played *Three Questions*?" Harrison asked incredulously.

"Played it? I've never even heard of it," she said in self-defense.

"Oh! We play it every time we have a do."

"A do?"

"Heck yeah! A sit-down do or a stand-up do. Don't matter any. *Three Questions* is the quickest way to break the ice. You'll see."

"I wasn't aware any ice needed breaking, but why not? I'm a good sport. How do you play?"

"Well," Harrison began, "each person has to think up three different questions and then write each one on a little slip of paper. See?" he said as he waved it slightly back and forth above his head.

"Harrison, I'm sure she knows a little slip of paper when she sees one," Cousin Duane ribbed.

"You're just bein' thorough, Harry. Don't let Cousin Duane give you any lip," I said.

He blushed.

"Go on," Lily encouraged.

"Well, then y'all drop 'em into a bowl…or a hat…or whathaveyou. Then someone jumbles them all together and when the container's passed around, people draw out *one* little slip a paper. Everyone has to answer."

"*Everyone?*" Lily asked.

"Everyone," Harrison replied. "Otherwise, ya hafta take a dare. An' I know from firsthand experience that the dares tend to be…well…unpleasant."

"Sheesh! It's the Swamp East version of *Truth or Dare*."

"*Truth or Dare?*" Harrison asked. "Never heard of it. I'll give y'all a couple a minutes."

❦ ❦ ❦

"All in? I'm ready to jumble 'em up."

"Just a sec," Lily said.

"Twelve to choose from. Lessee what I'll pull up out of this bag tonight."

(We had used Lily's canvas tote.) He pulled out the first question and read it out loud.

"What is the classiest thing you've ever witnessed?"

"It's *got* to be Lily's," I whispered after I leaned in toward Cousin Duane.

"I reckon I forgot ta mention that you don't need ta sign your name on the little slip of paper," Harrison explained.

A subtle "Oh!" escaped from Lily's lips.

❦ ❦ ❦

"I'm goin' first," Harrison announced.

"I was in Poplar Bluff with Dad not this Christmas, but last Christmas and we had gone into the Post Office to buy a book of postage stamps. This little old lady was standing at the counter, counting out nickels and pennies to buy a stamp. As she counted, she stacked each coin neatly on top of the one before till she had made herself a little tower of coins. Ha ha. I guess it musta rankled the young guy behind the counter, 'cause he slammed her stamp down on the counter."

"Jus' then somebody opened the front door of the lobby to come in and WHOOSH that stamp was airborne! We all watched it circle around and around the lobby till it finally landed right in the middle of the floor."

"That little old lady quietly went over to that stamp that was on the lobby floor, picked it up, and set the tower of coins in the exact spot. Everyone in the Post Office laughed. Well, everyone, that is, but the young guy behind the counter."

"My turn?" Lily asked.

"Yeah. We generally go clockwise," Harrison answered.

"Well." All eyes were on her and she was relishing every second of the attention. "Janelle was on leave and she took me to Kansas City…Missouri…to visit some of her old friends. They had all been nurses together in the Air Force. One of Janelle's friends had married Hugh Berensen…you know…he was governor of Missouri a while back."

"Janelle and I were invited to a brunch in his honor at Lite Bite in Crown Center. I had noticed a faint odor when we first went in but I just couldn't put my finger on what it was. I *knew* I'd recognized that smell from somewhere before. When I got a chance, I privately asked Isabelle, that's Janelle's friend who married the governor, if she knew what the smell was. And she said, 'It's probably just a little bug spray. I know a lot of the shops and eateries had the exterminators in on Sunday night. A friend of mine works upstairs in Hobby Haven and I'm in and out of there two or three times a week.'"

"It made sense. Like I said, it was just a faint odor. I'm very perceptive. The restaurant was nice and cozy and the food was excellent. I had the house special-spinach crepes and Kansas City Beef Stew. And the governor's assistant had caught my eye right away. She was immaculately dressed and groomed and seemed to hang, suspended on his every word. If I were Isabelle…I wouldn't have put up with that obvious flirting for one millisecond…but anyway, let me get to the classy part."

"Things couldn't have been any nicer and then…without warning…down from the grid ceiling panel dropped a bug, in the middle of its death throes. *And it landed right on the governor's left shoulder!* I suppose anybody else would've squealed and swatted at the thing, but not the governor's assistant. She calmly reached over and brushed the intruder off his shoulder like it was a stray hair or a flake of dandruff and then casually complimented him on how handsome he was looking that day. I don't know how many, if any, saw it. But *I* did and I thought...I'd witnessed pure class."

Lily leaned back in Dad's recliner, apparently pleased with herself.

"I don't rightly know how classy this is, but I saw it and I liked it and I'm gonna tell y'all," Cousin Duane said. "I was in St Louis, at Famous Barr. I was in there with Carter, a friend a mine and his fiancée, Claire, and we were standin' right beside the perfume counter."

"Fiancée," Lily mused. "That must be a euphemism for *pregnant girlfriend*."

"This man comes up and asks the salesclerk to see something in the fifteen-dollar range. 'I'd like to buy a gift for my mother-something really nice,' he said kinda soft. If I hadna been standin' right there, I couldna even made out what he was sayin'; it was so soft. The salesclerk put on airs and rolled her bug eyes at the man. 'I don't really have anything *that* cheap,' she said. The man looked at us and kinda melted inta hisself, like he was powerful embarrassed."

"Then he hung his head, like a whipped puppy and slouched on out of the store. Claire pulled that salesgirl up short when she leaned over the counter and whispered, 'I know that man. He works three jobs just so he can afford to keep his old mother in a decent nursing home.' That rude salesclerk's face turned beet-red. 'I...didn't...know. I just thought...he was some...cheapskate.'"

"Claire shot back, 'Well now you do. I'm going to march right down to the store manager's office and give him an earful. I'm going to tell him just how *unprofessional* you were to a potential customer. And you know something *else*? I am never spending one dime in this store again.'"

"Claire stomped out and we trailed right behind 'er. She followed through with her threat and reported the entire ugly episode to the store manager."

"When we finally got to the parking lot, I said, 'Of all the folks in St. Louis, *what're the odds* of you knowin' that man at the perfume counter?' Claire said, 'Oh! I didn't know him from a pile of lumber! I just wasn't lettin' no snobby bitch make him feel like a loser. Not on my watch.'"

A toothy smile broke out over Cousin Duane's handsome face.

"That Claire is one stand-up girl."

"Well…I would have told that salesgirl that the man *was* the manager of the store…disguised as a customer just to see the employees *in action*. No, on second thought…I would've told her…the man was the store*owner!* That would have been even better," Lily said.

"Dang, looks like nothin' classy ever happens 'round here. So far all these things happened somewhere else-Poplar Bluff, Kansas City, and St. Louis," Harrison complained.

"I have one that happened here…right here in Swamp East. And what makes it classy is that practically no one even knew what was goin' on."

"Oh, yeah?" Cousin Duane leaned in close, his curiosity primed.

"Yeah. It might spoil it if I used real names, so I'm jus' gonna tell ya what the person did, but not who the person is."

Everyone agreed.

"I knew a woman who didn't have much to speak of, but month after month she gave a little bit of it ta someone she reckoned needed it a lot more. The person she helped had just given birth to a small baby and didn't even have a job. Well, I met that baby a while back and now she is all but finished with medical school. And it happened right here…right here in good ol' Swamp East. Don't ya think that's pretty classy?"

"Tell us who it is," Lily urged.

"Nah."

"On ta question number two," Harrison announced.

"So now *I* get to draw first?" Lily inquired.

"Yep."

"Who was it, Flowerpot?" Cousin Duane whispered in my ear.

"Ask me again…some other time."

Lily reached in and pulled out a little slip of paper.

"What is the grossest thing you've ever done?" she read out loud.

"Gotta be Cousin Duane's!" I teased.

"Dudn't hafta be," he said.

"May I pass?" Lily whined. "I don't really go around doing gross things…on purpose. I just can't think of a single gross thing…"

"Why, a course ya can pass. But…don't forget…If ya pass, ya hafta take a dare," Harrison warned.

She sat for a good minute, dredging through her memory banks for something gross but not *too* gross. Something gross, but not humiliating.

"Okay. This one seems a likely candidate. Three summers ago, when Janelle was on leave and we were touring the Grand Canyon, we spent *way* more money than we had intended, so we didn't have enough to eat dinner that night. So…when nobody was looking…we sat down at a table where a big family with a lot of kids had just finished eating and there was still a pretty big mess. The busboys hadn't been around to clear it all away yet. We sat down and started scrounging through all of their leftovers. I was *so* hungry I scraped the jelly right out of the packet and ate it…without any toast! The waitress was totally confused and just about to report us to the restaurant manager, but Janelle gave her the most pitiful look I'd ever seen and the waitress let it go. Now…how's that for super gross?"

"Girl, that ain't nothin'. One winter I had a cash flow problem that ran so deep, I hadta use my own earwax for lip salve," Cousin Duane bragged.

I thought Lily was going to be ill.

"Your turn, Flowerpot."

"Well, I was in Uncle Richie's Café," I explained. "And one a the Miller's dogs came in and crapped right there in the middle of the floor."

"Ewww!" Lily emitted in protest.

"Yeah, and that *wasn't* the gross part," I continued.

Poor Lily, I could tell she wasn't used to such coarse talk. But that didn't stop me from finishing my story.

"That dog had worms…and there they were…mixed with all a that crap in a nasty heap on the floor. And the café was just chock-full of payin' customers. Uncle Richie frantically signaled me to come back into the kitchen. I did. And do you know that he promised me a crisp ten dollar bill if I'd clean the mess up quick?"

"Sheesh! Senga, tell me you didn't do it." Lily moaned. "That is exceedingly vile."

"For ten dollars? Heck ya! I woulda cleaned up *two* piles a dog crap for ten dollars."

"That's five dollars a pile. You're a gen-u-ine entrepreneur."

"Hmmm. You want gross? I'll give ya gross. I was at a family reunion picnic and Uncle Gordon asked me if I wanted a swig a his coke. We all knew that Uncle Gordon never drank his coke straight; It hadta have a spike a this or a spike a that. So I said sure thing. I took a great big swallow, thinkin' it was a big treat for a ten-year-old boy to get to sip a little liquor on the sly."

I thought I detected a slight green tinge as it passed over Harrison's face. The poor guy looked like he was done for.

"Are you all right, Harry?" I asked.

"Gah, Flowerpot! It weren't coke. He'd been using that cup…as a spittin' can for his chewin' tobacco!"

A collective groan rose from the three of us. It's one thing to be duped and quite another thing to be duped by a close and trusted relative.

"My turn."

Lily passed the canvas tote to Cousin Duane and he fished around till he latched on to a slip of paper.

"No fair," he grumbled. "This is two questions on one slip a paper."

"Let's hear 'em first and then we'll decide," Harrison suggested.

"Sounds fair enough. Okay…the first one asks, 'Do you believe in Heaven?' and the second one asks, 'If you do, *where* do you think Heaven is?'"

"Now that's funny," Cousin Duane said.

"What's so funny about it?" Lily demanded.

"I didn't mean it was a funny ha ha. I just meant it was funny, ya know the *timin'* is funny, 'cause I was jus' thinkin' 'bout that very thing this past summer. Gah! It was hot. Y'all remember how hot it was? I was at work and not a lot was goin' on, so I spent most of a half hour watchin' this fat fly crawl up the side of my desk."

"What is it you do?" Lily interrupted.

"I'm a physical therapist," Cousin Duane answered.

"This fly was so fat, he couldn'ta become airborne without a good, runnin' start. The air conditioner had given up the ghost first thing that mornin' and we were all dyin' in there. I'd plugged in this small fan and it was like one of those moments…when somethin' in the universe breaks loose and you catch a glimpse of somethin' bigger than yourself-somethin' grand. You know, Flowerpot, that word Gran always used when the dullness of life would suddenly crack open and cough up somethin' wonderful…somethin' unexpected."

"Serendipitous?"

"Yeah, Flowerpot. That's the word I was huntin' for. When I was watchin' that fan, that's when it came to me. It hit me like a bolt from the blue. The fan was on HIGH, so I couldn't see the blades, but I knew they were whirrin' like mad. I knew they was there. And jus' ta make sure they were still there, I poked the eraser end of my pencil in half a dozen times just for the hell of it. Like I told ya, it was blazin' hot and there wasn't anything to do. And I remember thinkin', 'I reckon that's just how Heaven is. It's been right here all along, just a pencil poke away, only it's whirrin' so fast…so full a energy…that none of us can see it.'"

"Who knows? Maybe this here room…is full ta splittin' with spirits. We may be surrounded by an audience and not even know it."

The hair stood up on the back of my neck.

Cousin Duane continued. "Then I switched the fan down to MEDIUM. I still couldn't see those blades, but I reckoned I had a far better chance a seein' 'em since they were movin' so much slower. And I imagined I could, when I squinched my eyes together a bit."

"Ya ever known any *special people*-the kinda folks who seem to have an eye on the bigger picture? They know things they have no business knowin'. They know things that are physically impossible for them to know, 'cause they never been anyplace or really done anything. But all of a sudden this important stuff just seems to pop into their heads."

He turned toward me.

"Flowerpot, I know *you* know what I mean. Ya know Gran was like that."

(Gran *was* like that. But since I'd been around her my entire life, I thought it was the way *all* grandmothers were. It wasn't till I was in high school and started spending time with some of the residents at the nursing home that I realized she was different.)

"Some people jus' seem to move on their hunches and intuition. I'm not talkin' about no crazy folks…who hear voices and walk down the street mutterin' to themselves and battin' at invisible pests. And I'm not talkin' about those screwball psychics some folks hire for dinner parties."

"I believe there are people who are tuned in, an' more sensitive to what's goin' on. Those are the folks who could see the fan blades spinnin' on medium. Folks sometimes get to lift the veil we're all livin' under and…for a little while at least…get to steal a glance at somethin' bigger."

"Then I switched the blades to OFF. They slowed down and stopped. And I saw them plain as day…those unyieldin', hard plastic blades. And that's where the bulk of us mere mortals live. We only believe what we can see...what we can handle with our own two hands...and what is sittin' right in front of our faces."

Nobody said a word.

"Yeah, I believe in Heaven," Cousin Duane confided. "An' I believe it's right here, closer to us 'en most people even consider."

"Yeah, I believe too. I always reckoned it was somewhere up in the sky," I said.

"Me too," Harrison agreed.

"Same here," Lily quickly added.

"Your turn," Harrison said with a boyish smile.

I slipped my hand into the tote and pulled out a promising slip of paper.

"What is your worst fear?" I read out loud.

I crumpled the slip of paper up and tossed it onto the coffee table.

"Well, up till last night, I woulda said hands-down the most horrible thing in the world would hafta be drowning. But I jus' don't feel like that anymore. So I'm gonna hafta say...fallin' under a speedin' train. Or bein' attacked by a shark. I reckon' they about tie in my mind."

"There's not a lot of sharks kickin' about in southeast Missouri, Flowerpot, so looks like you won't have ta worry," Cousin Duane joked.

"My biggest fear?" Harrison asked. "My biggest fear is that Senga would run off...an' become a nun and decide not to marry me after I've waited all these years."

"I'd never do that to you, Harry, so put your fear to rest," I assured him.

Lily looked uncomfortable, like a thousand needles were pricking into her backside from the chair.

"Sheesh! Okay. I've never told anybody this...but here goes. My worst fear...is that it's the very first day...and I'm at *another* new school. Either Janelle has forgotten to register me or she has...and some knucklehead in the office loses all of my paperwork...and my name isn't on the list. So there I am…I'm standing there…waiting…and all of the other students are busy heading off to their first period and I'm left standing in the hallway…with no place to go."

"Has that ever happened to you?" Cousin Duane asked tenderly.

"No, it hasn't," Lily answered.

He reached over and took her hand.

"Good."

She smiled.

"I guess my worst fear is that one a these days, I'll get up an' look in the mirror an' I'll see the face of some decrepit old man a starin' back at me. I been so lonely since Mom died. I have no one ta look after but myself, an' I ain't really what anybody would call a high-maintenance man."

🍁 🍁 🍁

"So why do people call you Cousin Duane? Why not…just Duane?"

"Because we *do* for family."

"I don't understand," Lily said.

"It was really Flowerpot's brothers who first thought it up. The first day I started kindergarten…my mom proudly walked me to school…and a handful a jerkweeds gave me hell over it."

"Why did they do that?" Lily asked.

"I guess my mom was acting funny or something. I can't remember. Whenever my mom got real excited about something, she did tend to act kinda funny."

"Funny, like…?"

She shrugged, encouraging Cousin Duane to respond.

"Lily…my mom was mentally retarded."

"Oh."

"And when Flowerpot's big brothers…Bill, Barry, and Larry heard about it, they walked me to school every single day…and introduced me to everyone as *Cousin Duane*. You can bet that I didn't have one ounce of grief after that."

"And why not? What difference could that possibly have made?" Lily asked.

"'Cause *nobody* messed with the Tait Brothers."

"O-oh," she said, with a new understanding of the situation.

"I kinda go by C.D. nowadays."

Lily nodded.

"C. D. I like that," she said.

"I know what you must be thinkin'," Cousin Duane confided in a low tone. "And the answer is no…I'm not mental. Ya see…when my mom was being born, the umbilical cord wrapped itself around her neck jus' long enough to cut off her air. It wasn't somethin'…she coulda passed on to me. In fact…I graduated top a my class."

"Oh! I didn't think…"

But he smiled at her. He'd heard it all before.

"And for the record…I was just messin' with ya…'bout the earwax."

🍁   🍁   🍁

Wearing our winter coats, we slow danced on the back porch. And the stars winked at us, incandescent eyes in a black velvet face.

March

"WELL, WHAT WOULD YOU HAVE SAID?" Lily repeated.

🍁   🍁   🍁

"Why're ya askin' me that for?"
"You forgot to take the rest of the little slips of paper out of my canvas tote."
"Huh?"
"I read the other eight questions. You remember. The questions…from that game we played…The ones we never picked were still in my canvas tote."
"Oh! Yeah."
"Well…I read the other eight questions. I was just…I was just wondering…"
Lily carefully stepped around the puddle that had swollen to fill the collapsed sidewalk.
"What?" I asked.
"I was just wondering…what would you have said if someone had pulled out the question, 'WHO IS YOUR BEST FRIEND?'"
Without hesitation, I answered. "I woulda said, *Lily*. Who else?"
"Well…what about Harrison?"
"What about Harrison?"

"He seems convinced that he's going to marry you…once you've both graduated from college."

"And he is. We are gonna get married. We're gonna get married just as soon as we both graduate from college. Not one day before and not one day after."

"Isn't *he* your best friend?" Lily asked quietly, as if she were on tenterhooks.

"Harrison? Nah! He's my boyfriend and one a these days he's gonna be my husband, so he doesn't count."

In my peripheral vision, I took in Lily's profile. She was smiling.

"I have something to confess," she said.

"Yeah? What is it?"

"That game we played…"

"*Three Questions?*"

"Yes."

"What about it?" I asked.

"I wasn't exactly…truthful…when I answered one of the questions."

"You mean…*you lied*?" I asked in my most accusing voice.

"It was just a game, Senga. I just thought…"

I clutched her arm and wheeled her around so that she was facing me.

"It was just a game…" she repeated.

"I was jus' messin' with ya, Lily. Hell! I lied too!"

"Senga! How could you jerk me around like that? You nearly scared me to death."

"And you're right. It's just a game. Gran always told me to keep my heart with all confidence. Game or no game, some secrets are meant to be kept."

"I'll tell you what I lied about…if you tell me," Lily bargained.

"It's a deal."

"The question about Heaven…it was mine. I agreed with you and Harrison, but I…I really don't believe in Heaven at all. I've *tried* to believe, honest I have. I just haven't been able to convince myself that there is anything else…besides what I can see with my own two eyes. How did C.D. put it? *'We only believe what we can see…what we can handle with our own two hands…what is sittin' right in front of our faces.'*"

"But after Gran died, you said…"

"I was just trying to comfort you. You were so-acting so…*morbid*…about your gran. I figured that's what a friend would say," Lily explained.

"It's okay, Lily."

"Now you have to tell me which question you lied about," Lily reminded.

"It was the one about my biggest fear. I don't really give two hoots about fallin' under some speedin' train or bein' chum for a hungry shark in the middle of a feedin' frenzy. Gah! I'm just afraid…that one day…Harry'll snap out of it and decide I'm not the one he loves after all."

"That's crazy talk, Senga. It's obvious to everybody that he adores you."

"I know. Only…there's this cold doubt that lurks…in some dark corner of my soul. Every now and again it rears its ugly head…and reminds me…that even in the most beautimus wedding dress, I'm still just a plain, overall-wearin' kinda girl underneath."

Lily laughed out loud.

"Oh! And the question about the grossest thing you'd ever done…it *wasn't* C.D.'s."

"Then who's was it?"

"It was Harrison's."

"How'dja know that?"

"After I dumped all of the questions out and read them, I compared handwriting samples. And don't forget…I know how Harrison, you, and I all write. It was your Harry's all right."

"Unless...somebody was disguising his or her handwriting," I suggested.

"Would somebody do that?" she asked in astonishment.

"Nobody I know. You're a regular gumshoe, Lily."

❦   ❦   ❦

"I have a little surprise for you."

"Yeah? What is it?"

"The better question would be, 'Who is it?'"

I was stumped.

"Janelle's been babysitting an adorable little boy named Mitchell all week."

"Adorable?" I couldn't believe my ears. "You told me you hated babies."

"Oh! I do. I only said adorable for your benefit. Living in Swamp East all your life, I naturally figured you for the baby loving type. I can't stand them myself."

How anybody could hate a baby was beyond me. So I simply refused to believe that she actually *hated* all of them; she probably just hadn't ever been around one long enough to get used to it.

"Whaddaya have against babies anyhow?" I asked. "Why *don't* you like them?"

"Because."

"That's no answer."

"For one thing, they're just *so* needy. They seem to believe that they are the very center of the universe. Sheesh! When you get near one you can almost hear a faint whirring sound, like the world spinning on its axis. And for another...people start acting stupid whenever a baby is around."

"Whaddaya mean?" I asked.

"Haven't you ever noticed how people act whenever a baby pops up?"

"I guess not."

"It's absolutely horrid. And I'm not talking about some slack jawed yokels who barely have four teeth to grind together with a pack of children of their own. No, I'm talking about college educated, articulate, change-their-underwear-every-single-day people. People who read *Newsweek*, write novels, and are doctors' wives. It's as if they descend a rung or two down the evolutionary ladder whenever they come into direct contact with a baby. And the most inane things start pouring out of their mouths."

She put her face inches from mine and cooed, "'What a cutie patootie you are. *Yes*, you are! Yes, *you* are! Is that nana yummy nummy nummy?'"

She screwed up her face and added, "It's nauseating!"

"I think it's kinda cute." I said.

"I suppose you would. Anyway…we're going to have to be quiet. Mitchell takes his nap around this time of day."

No one heard Lily unlock the front door, and no one heard our careful footsteps on the vestibule's parquet tile. I eased onto the cracked, comfortable leather couch, (Lily always referred to it as "the sofa.") and had just started to lug my binder from my backpack when the baby monitor crackled to life.

Lily put a finger to her lips, signaling me to keep quiet.

"I thought he would *never* stop crying!" an unfamiliar voice softly said. "You really have a knack for this motherhood stuff."

"Well, Lil was only five months old when she came to live with me. I guess you might say…I had a crash course."

I recognized Janelle's voice.

"I've never liked babies myself," the stranger confided.

"Then why did you have him?"

"Davis wanted a son. Besides…Mitchell won't stay little and creepy like this forever." The woman added, "But I have to admit…he does look adorable when he's asleep…all curled up next to his teddy bear. I want to thank you again for keeping him all week. It's the first real break I've had since he was born."

"Oh! It was fun."

"Who could've guessed that we'd wind up living so close to each other after all these years?"

"Just the luck of the draw," Janelle said.

And they giggled-the way girls do at slumber parties or the way women do who have weathered a storm together.

"I mean it. Anytime you need a little break, just give me a call and I'll be glad to have him over. He reminds me of Lil when she was that age. She was completely beautiful."

Upon hearing this Lily put on an insouciant smirk.

"Are you okay...not having any children?"

"I have *Lily*."

Janelle's voice took on an edgy quality that I'd never heard before.

"I'm sorry. What I meant was...any children *of your own*. I always thought you and Ted would've had some. You were married five years. Right?"

"Yeah. Five years. But Ted never wanted any kids."

"How'd he handle it when Lily came to live with you?"

"He was fine...at first. I guess he thought it was just going to be...some temporary thing. But the morning I held that document in my hand...the morning the adoption was final...he changed. He packed up everything he owned and was gone that afternoon."

"WHAT A JERK! Oh! Nelly, I'm *so* sorry."

"It's okay. I wouldn't have traded Lily Billy for ten *thousand* Ted's!"

The monitor fell silent and I didn't dare look at Lily. I knew instinctively that I had just heard something that I was never meant to hear. I wanted to vanish.

"How much does she know?" the unfamiliar voice asked.

"Not much," Janelle replied. "I just thought...I could wait...She'd already been through so much. And she was always...such a *sensitive* child...You know...I used to read to her when she was little...every night that I was home. And I had been reading *Sleeping Beauty*. And this...particular version had only one picture. I have never forgotten the look...on Lily Billy's little face when she saw the picture in that book. Sleeping Beauty was this beautiful, blue-eyed, flaxen-haired princess, and...when Lil saw that picture, she burst into tears. At first, I couldn't understand why she was crying. I thought maybe it was because she couldn't bear to see Sleeping Beauty asleep for so long, looking so helpless...but it wasn't that at all. It never would've dawned on me..."

"Why was she crying?"

"I got her to calm down. And that's when she told me. You see...every night that I had been reading...Lil had been forming this little picture...in her mind...of just how the beautiful, sleeping princess ought to look. And she had imagined a beautiful Filipina princess with long black hair, brown eyes, and brown skin...a princess who looked just like *her*. Then I understood...It finally began to make some sense..."

"Well, what was it she said to you?"

"She looked up at me with her marvelous brown eyes and asked, 'Does Sleeping Beauty *have* to look like that?'"

"She took the book out of my hands and closed it...She squeezed it into her bookshelf with all of the other books...and never allowed me to read to her again."

"That does sound like a sensitive little girl."

"You have no idea," Janelle said softly.

"But sensitive or not...you had to have told her..."

"I..."

"You mean...you *never* told her?"

"I meant to...I meant to, Cathy....I am *so* tired of feeling guilty over the whole thing. All these years and I still have this tremendous load of guilt."

"Why? It wasn't your fault. Nobody knew he was going to do that. You couldn't have known. Hell! I couldn't have guessed in a million years he was capable of something like that. And you certainly couldn't have done anything to stop him! He was stationed in California and you were stationed clear over in New Jersey."

"I know…I know all that…"

"You have to stop beating yourself up all of the time over something you didn't cause and couldn't have prevented. It's killing you, Nelly! Can't you see that?"

"I just wish…"

"If it hadn't been for you, she probably would've bounced around from foster home to foster home. And what kind of life would that have been for a little girl?"

"I flew down as soon as I could…"

"I know you did."

"I can still see her. Oh, Cathy! That little bandaged stump of a leg flailing in the air…those little fists clenched, jerking back and forth…"

"Stop it. Stop it, Nelly," Cathy pleaded.

"And…I could never…say *no* to her. I couldn't deny her anything…not after all she'd already been through…"

"I'm sure you did the best you could. Hell, that's all any of us can do. And look at her. She's turned out fine. She's smart…and exquisitely beautiful. You really should learn to choose your battles, you know. You need to save your strength for taking a baseball bat to all of the young guys who are going to be trying to date her. She is an exceptional young woman," the woman said.

Although that was a pile of compliments, I knew better than to glance over at Lily. I couldn't bear to see her trademark smirk replaced with something forlorn, or worse yet, something ugly.

"Cathy…I've bought Lily Billy…a crapload of stuff over the years…to try and make up…I just couldn't face her."

Janelle was crying now. Her words came in fits and starts between great gusts of emotion.

"I even...I'm so ashamed to admit it to you. I even *volunteered* to go on TDY's just to get away from Lily's accusing little face."

"Lily didn't have an accusing face. Nelly, you're the only mother she's ever known."

"Sometimes...when a secret is kept too long...it just becomes...impossible to explain. Why do you think...I've never taken her back to Billerica? I couldn't risk some fool telling her. I couldn't bear that. She couldn't bear that. I think...she should hear it from me...before she hears it from somebody else."

I stared hard at Lily's back as she walked out of the living room. I reckoned I could've been out of that front door like a shot if I just could've made my move. *"Legs, don't fail me now!"* I thought to myself, but my body was heavy as lead and I had missed my only opportunity to escape.

"Senga, get in here!" Lily ordered.

I felt ill. No good would come of this.

Janelle was sitting cross-legged in Mitchell's playpen, clutching a half-empty bottle of sloe gin to her breast. She looked ripping drunk.

"Do you have something you'd like to tell me?" Lily demanded.

"Not now," Janelle replied.

Lily stubbornly stamped her foot on the floor.

"Oh! So you can tell Cathy, but you can't tell me! Is that how it is?"

"I think...we should wait...till we're alone."

"Don't worry, Janelle. Anything you have to say to me, you can say in front of Senga."

"I think I'm going to be sick," Janelle moaned.

"I'm not leaving this room until you tell me."

Janelle still couldn't refuse Lily anything.

"I meant...to tell you. I just wanted..."

"Oh sheesh! Why even bother with the truth when a lie is so much more convenient!"

Janelle blanched at Lily's scalding remark.

"It might be better...if you read it for yourself. The key's in the chest."

"What chest?" Lily demanded.

"The treasure chest."

Janelle pointed unsteadily toward the fish tank that hugged the far wall.

Lily pushed up her sweater sleeve, plunged her arm into the aquarium, and pulled out the miniature treasure chest. She carefully pried it open. There was the key. She removed it from its wet hiding place and wiped it on her jeans. She held it up in the air and waved it back and forth as she glared at Janelle.

"I'm...going to be sick," Janelle heaved.

"What is this the key for?"

"The fire safe...it's under my bed."

"I *know* where it is," Lily snapped.

Lily pulled the fire safe from under Janelle's bed. She quickly unlocked it. I couldn't help wondering what she was looking for; what she was in such an all-fired hurry to find. She sat very still on the edge of the bed. Then she methodically searched the safe's contents. I watched as she pulled out a neat bundle of yellowed newspaper clippings.

"Owwww."

Cathy pulled Janelle's limp body from the playpen and half dragged her to the bathroom. She held her hair back so it wouldn't snag any of the vomit on its way to the toilet.

I reckoned that must be the acid test of friendship.

❦   ❦   ❦

The first article was a hometown news release with headlines that read:

KEEPING IT IN THE FAMILY
Mann twins join the
United States Air Force

And there were individual photographs of a young man and a young woman in Air Force dress blues. They both looked like pale, watered down versions of Lily. And beneath each photograph, a name was printed-

John Austin Mann and Janelle Rae Mann.

I immediately recognized the photograph of the young man. It was the same pose as the photo in the frame on Lily's nightstand. It was her dad. Then I stared hard and couldn't peel my eyes off the photograph of the young woman.

"Janelle…is your…*aunt?*" I asked incredulously.

But Lily didn't answer.

The next clipping read:

INFANT IN STABLE CONDITION

We read that article in silence. My heart ached for the little baby described in that article. My heart broke because I knew it was Lily.

Then she picked a lengthy article. This one was cut from some military newspaper:

LT. MANN INDICTED IN CHILD ABUSE CASE

It was all there-the accusation, dishonorable discharge, and imprisonment. I felt horrible for Lily. Parents were supposed to *protect* their children. And her dad had done this.

Lily sat quietly on the edge of Janelle's bed. The entire time we'd read, she'd never uttered so much as a sigh. She never shifted her weight or even changed her facial expression.

I watched as she tentatively fingered an envelope. It was pale pink with two words scrawled in tight, little letters on its front:

Talitha Koum.

I watched as she carefully opened it. I was terrified that some little scrap of the past would tumble out, something so hideous that Lily might read it and never be the same. I was relieved when Lily found only a small piece of paper tucked inside. It read-Total Deposit—$2,112.10 (at ten cents a whack).

"What does that mean?" I asked.

But Lily didn't answer.

I couldn't bear any more, so I sat, without speaking, as Lily re-read every one of those awful clippings. And the painful silence was punctuated by the sound of Janelle's intermittent retching in the bathroom.

April

"I thought you didn't like animals," I said.

"I don't."

"Then…why…do you insist on feeding him?"

"Whenever it was my turn…I taught him a little trick."

"Really? I didn't realize you could teach a rat a little trick."

"Oh! They're a lot smarter than mice," Lily admitted.

I reckoned that wasn't saying much. Just how smart does the average mouse have to be?

"So…what trick did you manage to teach him?"

"…to stand on his two hind legs, turn around twice, and reach out for his food. It's really cute."

"I'm sure it is."

"But I can't feed him now."

"Why not?" I asked.

I tapped against the side of the wire cage. I'd grown fond of Timmy, the rat of our class project.

"Sure you can. You have plenty of rat chow left."

"Nobody's watching," Lily whispered.

"What?"

"Nobody's watching," she repeated so softly that I could barely hear.

"Well, what difference does that make?" I asked.

"Someone *has* to be watching."

I reckoned Lily was destined to be in the spotlight; her need for an audience seemed especially desperate and naked.

🍁   🍁   🍁

"*Learn anything?*" Mrs. Lessing asked.

A collective groan rose from the students. And just as quickly, the class fell silent. We had learned what that phrase meant on a Monday morning.

"Pop Quiz! Take out a sheet of paper and a pencil and put everything else under your desks. I want you to write…um…about a page will do…on what you learned from the rat project. Now listen up, budding scientists. You are to list the constants, the variables, the results, and how similar circumstances might effect human beings. Are there any questions?"

"Yeah. Is this quiz gonna be hard?" It was some wiseacre from the back row.

"Not if you know the answers," Mrs. Lessing quipped.

"Are there any *real* questions? I didn't think so. You may take the entire class period if you need to. You may begin."

🍁   🍁   🍁

"How'dja do?"

"It was a piece of cake," Lily bragged. "Science has always been a snap for me. So orderly, you know?"

"I reckon. Gran said that I must have a photographic memory, 'cause I can read somethin' one time and always remember it. That doesn't mean I always understand it, but I can spew it out easy as pie whenever a test comes up."

"Lucky you. I only wish archery were that simple," Lily complained.

"Ah, you'll get the hang of it. Ms. Parenti is determined to put some real meat on those bony arms of yours," I said with a half smile.

"That sounds particularly vile, doesn't it?"

"What does?"

"Meaty arms. How many women movie stars or news announcers do you see with meaty arms?"

"Not many, I reckon."

"That's right, Senga. And you're not likely to see any in the near future either."

I watched her gather her hair into a soft ponytail and then bend to drink from the water fountain. She took her time. Lily wasn't the sort to look behind her. She was used to looking forward; used to being the one who garnered all of the attention, all of the admiring glances. I saw *her* as this exquisite doll and the *rest of us* were merely the Styrofoam peanuts that kept her from jostling and cracking on her journey through life.

Our district had to have four entire years of physical education in high school. Superintendent Palmer had made it that way on account of all the chunky bodies that clogged his hallowed halls. It was bad enough that he looked like Ichabod Crane. Now he wanted us to be pinched and gaunt and angular so that we looked like him too.

Lily had read an article to me out of one of Janelle's nursing magazines. The headlines blared,

AMERICA'S YOUTH-
AN OBESITY EPIDEMIC?

It went on to explain how nearly two-thirds of our nation's young people were overweight, due primarily to our lack of regular, physical activity. Superintendent Palmer must've read that very same article. He was vigilant as any drill sergeant as he waged his not so private war on cellulite.

❦   ❦   ❦

We were changing into our gym clothes when she appeared. She had been absent nine days of school. And that was a lot. If a student missed ten or more days in any one semester, no credit was given and that's as good as failing. She looked extra pale and even without trying, I couldn't help noticing the telltale signs of bruises that were in various stages of healing…the faintest of purples and a sickeningly sallow green.

"Missed ya at the Valentine Dance," she said.

Lily and I pretended not to hear.

"Hey! I'm talkin' ta you!" Red erupted.

"What did you say?" Lily asked.

"Wasn't talkin' ta no Jap."

"Well I'm talking to *you*," Lily said matter-of-factly.

I knew no good would come of this.

"Missed ya at the Valentine Dance," Red repeated. "Where *were* ya, Senga?" she demanded. Even her hair seemed angry, like some deranged bird's nest constructed out of rusty Brillo pads.

"I stayed home."

As far as Lily was concerned, the conversation was already over.

"You want to eat dinner with us tonight? Janelle's fixing her world famous lasagna," Lily tempted. "And she makes one mean antipasto salad."

Before I could answer, Red had shoved Lily over the bench.

POP!

We all heard the sound, but only Lily understood its significance. Her eyes narrowed to slits as the color drained from her face. The metal fastener on her prosthesis had snapped, letting her stockinetted stump pull free.

"We-ll…ladies…What do we have here?" Red asked contemptuously.

She wasted no time snatching Lily's prosthetic foot. Then she held it high over her head, the way a prizefighter might proudly display his newly acquired belt. "Look-i-loo!"

"You horrible bitch!" Lily screamed. "You give that back to me this instant, or I'll…"

"You'll what?"

Lily quickly scrambled to an upright position.

"I'll tear you to pieces!" She shrieked.

Then she lunged at Red who nonchalantly tossed the prosthesis to Trish. She eagerly caught it and made a motion like she was going to pass it to Jazz. But Jazz lowered her gaze, galvanized by her companions' most recent devilment, and bolted out of the girls' locker room as fast as her legs could carry her.

"Give Lily her foot back, Red," I insisted. "And just leave her out of this. This has nothing to do with her. I *know* you hate me. And I know *why*. So if you wanna say somethin' to me, here I am. Just say it."

Trish chortled as she flipped the prosthetic foot back to Red.

"Oh! I'm gonna say it all right. I'm gonna make my point," Red announced. "You can count on that."

All my fear of Red and more fears for my future than I could begin to name welled up inside me.

Red glared at me through jaundiced eyes.

That's when she pulled the gun out of her backpack. My heart leapt. I thought it smacked hard into my ribs. She pointed the barrel directly at me and…with complete satisfaction…smiled.

"I missed ya at the Valentine Dance."

POP!

I will never understand why Lily jumped in front of me that afternoon.

❦   ❦   ❦

A nameless, faceless thing descended on Lily. And she hugged her knees into her chest and rocked back and forth in an impossibly tight ball.

Ms. Parenti, the gym teacher, had suddenly appeared, along with an audience of gawking, partially clad girls. Jazz burst through the double doors of the girls' locker room followed by Superintendent Palmer.

❦   ❦   ❦

I had the distinct impression she was repeating herself.

"Can I do *anything* to help?" Jazz asked again.

I wanted to say, "I think you've already done enough." But I didn't.

Instead, I looked up at her tear stained face. She had finally stood up to Red. I knew she always had it in her. She wasn't a bad person, just scared, like the rest of us. But I had completely misjudged Trish.

❦   ❦   ❦

"What did you say, Lily?"

"What is it about me that makes people want to hurt me?" she asked in a sepulchral tone.

I held her close in my arms.

"Not a thing, Lily. Not one thing."

I slicked back the stray hair that stuck resolutely to her clammy forehead and I gazed down into her soft, brown eyes. But she wasn't looking *at* me. She seemed to be looking right *through* me and it sent chills through my entire body.

"Ooooh!…Look at me…Senga…I'm shaking."

🍁   🍁   🍁

"THIS ISN'T OVER!" Red snarled.

It took both Superintendent Palmer and Ms. Parenti to drag her flailing body from the girls' locker room.

"THIS ISN'T OVER, SENGA TAIT!"

🍁   🍁   🍁

It was for Lily.

May

I reckon I gave the shortest valedictory speech in history. And one by one, as our names were called, we received our diplomas. Before descending the stage stairs, we each pulled a single, red rose from the massive vase. It had been our school's tradition for as long as any of us could remember. Each graduate took a rose out to the audience and handed it to that person who had been on the sidelines for the last four years, silently cheering them on. Almost everyone gave their rose to their parents. It was a funny thing to watch. The mothers hugged and cried-didn't matter if it was a son or a daughter. The fathers hugged their daughters, but stood straight and tall and shook hands with their sons or whacked them soundly on their backs.

I took two roses.

I gave one to Dad.

🍁   🍁   🍁

"I could never get Lil to step foot in there," Janelle admitted as she looked toward Uncle Richie's Café.
I smiled.
"Neither could I. She always called it the…"
"-The Chip-a-Tooth-Café," Janelle finished.
It was good to see her smile again.

"Lily had a way with words," I said.

"That she did."

We sat in awkward silence for a minute or so.

"I have somethin' for ya."

I handed her the rose and explained our school's tradition.

"That was thoughtful," she said dully.

"I reckoned ya wouldn't wanna go."

"Well, you were right. I probably *should* have gone. But I just couldn't force myself to do it. I just kept asking myself, 'What's the use, anyway?'"

"It was a nice graduation."

Janelle didn't say anything.

"But I guess if you've seen one, you've seen 'em all."

"I just couldn't be there…I…" She broke off, mid-sentence.

"It's okay, Janelle."

※ ※ ※

"Lily's funeral was beautiful," I said. (And I hoped it was. But my mind had been too numb to fasten on to anything and the entire morning had passed before me like the tail end of a bad dream.)

"Thank you," Janelle responded.

I had been the only student invited to Lily's funeral because, Janelle had whispered in my ear, I had been Lily's best friend. Apart from Harrison and Cousin Duane, I was Lily's *only* friend. But Janelle didn't need to hear that.

Not now.

Not ever.

I closed my eyes.

※ ※ ※

I wanted to see her. I had to see her, so I forced myself forward one step at a time. Would she be gray and waxy the way Aunt Gladys and

Gran had been? Would she even look like the Lily that had become my closest friend? I edged closer. She lay less than a foot away, close enough...to reach out...and touch. I wanted to be there, but at that same instant I wished I could fly away.

Stacked up beside the rest of my life, this was only a moment in time. I saw all this in a flash; but the entire scene-Lily, her casket, her expression-they were permanently seared into my memory. And whether real or imagined, I glimpsed an insouciant smirk on her face, like she was in on some wicked secret that the rest of us could only wonder at, but never know.

Branches, like gnarled fingers, scratched at a pastel sky. When that first clod of damp earth struck Lily's casket, Janelle seized me and held me close the way she might once have held Lily and cried so hard, that her powerful body jerked. It wasn't easy to breathe in her vise. And for a minute, I was terrified that she might let go.

He had been there. Up the embankment, obscured by the tree row. He'd swapped his usual BDU jacket for a shiny black suit. (I reckoned it musta been extraordinarily cheap to shine like that.) I wanted to punish him. I wanted to dash up there and tear him to pieces. In a way, all of this was really his fault...at least partly. Wasn't he the one who started the entire thing? Wasn't he the one who first wounded Lily? Fortunately for him, I rarely acted on my first impulse. For if I had, I would've wound up in the Hillcrest Home for Wayward Girls a long, long time ago.

I don't know how long I stared at him. Or if he even noticed.

Whatever it is that makes a man stand up straight and tall, every drop of it must of leaked out of that pitiful man, lurking among the trees, stoop shouldered and spent. What a burden it must've been for him to carry. Knowing he was the cause of something so ugly, the one responsible for ruining something that he could never fix. He had seen the better path, but had chosen the worse. His love for Lily had kept him watching over her all these years and had led him to her final resting-

place. But his shame had kept him rooted in the background, like some morbid spectator.

I felt sorry for him then. He had lost his only child and that seemed punishment enough.

🍁   🍁   🍁

I opened my eyes and saw the sun as it peeked from behind a troop of angry clouds.

"Did he love Lily?" I asked.

"Of course he did, Senga. He was Lily's *father*."

"Still...It was a hideous thing to do."

"I know it was. It was hideous. I wouldn't dare make any excuse for what he did; I wouldn't dream of defending him. But I know...he would've done *anything* in his power to undo that night, that five minutes that changed the rest of his life."

"And Lily's," I added.

"And Lily's," Janelle repeated. "He didn't love her the way she deserved to be loved, but he loved her the best he could. He was drunk that night...drunk out of his mind...and so *jealous* of Cora. That was Lily's mother."

"I know. Lily showed me a photograph of her."

"He couldn't stand Cora having any friends of her own. You know, the whole thing really wasn't even about Lily at all. It was about rage. It was about controlling another human being and wanting something he couldn't have." Janelle looked at me and smiled. "Did she ever figure out it was him?"

"I don't think so. I kept waiting for Lily to say something...to say *anything*...about what she'd read in those awful newspaper clippings that afternoon. Maybe if she would've talked about it, it might've been a key to what was goin' on in her mind. If she did know it...she never let on. She never said a word."

❦ ❦ ❦

Janelle nodded pensively and then she asked, "Are you *sure* about this, Senga?"

"As sure as I am about anything. Harrison will transfer up there after his first semester."

"What about your father?"

"He'll be okay," I said.

And in my heart of hearts I knew that he would make out just fine.

"It might be a little rough…in the beginning."

"What is he going to do?"

"He's sellin' out."

"That's too bad," Janelle responded.

"Nah. We both knew he wouldn't farm forever. It's not easy on a family farm to compete against the big guys."

She nodded in sympathy.

"Besides, he always had his business degree to fall back on. And ya know…I'm really proud a him. He's finally takin' the plunge and that takes a lot of guts."

I could see so much of Lily in Janelle. She even raised her left eyebrow when she was mullin' over somethin' important or waitin' for the answer to some question.

"To Boston then?" she asked.

"To Boston!" I replied.

I fastened my seat belt. Huge drops of rain pelted the car as I gazed out of my window. Was it just the luck of the draw as Lily had once told me? Or had some unseen hand thrust Lily and me together? It was the school year that *everything* happened, in the middle of nowhere, forty miles from Poplar Bluff.

About the Author

Rachel J. Ross enjoyed a stint in the Air Force reserves as an aeromedical evacuation technician. She later went on active duty as a medical services specialist.

She has a B.S. in elementary education and works as a long-term substitute.

Her other works include *The Locust Years* and *The Wonder Horse: A Collection of Poetry.*

She is currently residing in rural North Dakota.

0-595-21661-7